PASSIONTIDE

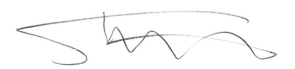

# PASSIONTIDE

A novel by Stephen Earley

© Stephen Earley 2002

ISBN 1-903314-33-X

All rights reserved. No part of this book may be reproduced or transmitted in any form or by any means, electronic or mechanical, including photocopying, recording, or by any information storage and retrieval system, without permission in writing from the publisher.

Published with the financial support of the
Arts Council of Wales

St. Alphonsus, *The Stations of the Cross*, Catholic Truth Society.
Edward Thomas, 'Rain', *Poems*, 1917.

Cover: A Welsh Wood, 1963. Photo, Julian Gough

Published and Printed by
Gwasg Pantycelyn, Lôn Ddewi, Caernarfon, Gwynedd LL55 1ER.
Printed in Wales

For Jane

Take a flat map, a globe *in plano*, and here is east and there is west as far asunder as two points can be put. But reduce this flat map to roundness, which is the true form, and then east and west touch one another, and all are one. So consider man's life aright to be a circle, *Pulvis es* and *in pulverem reverteris*, 'Dust thou art and to dust thou must return'; *nudus egressus, nudus revertar*, 'Naked I came, and naked I must go'; in this circle, the two points meet, the womb and the grave are but one point, they make but one station, there is but a step from that to this .

*John Donne.*

# Prologue

It was strange, the doctor thought, how those stupid bricks always looked so fresh and new when you approached them through the woods. What was it now? Thirty or more years since they were built? Cheap breeze-blocks and industry cement, put up hastily by bored city workmen, over an iron-working entrance of voluptuous limestone which took you back through the ages to Roman times. What a sin! Nature seemed to recognise it in those few paltry straggles of ivy and fern which hung down. Nothing stayed for long here. No stem clung, took root.

Geraint Morris finally reached the spot, touched the surface of the bricks. They were perfectly dry, which was odd because this was one of those late November days when everything, including his socks and muffler, seemed soaked up with thick Welsh rain. It was a steep and slippery slope to the spot. Dr Morris sat on a tree-stump to get his breathe back. There, just above a feathery tree-line of young birch, was the dark outline of Penlan hill. Few people climbed it these days. And the only vehicles that took the narrow mountain road, if the local press was to be believed, were drug-pushers from down in the Bay, choosing rural desolation to make their midnight deals. Long gone were all those lovers in their Ford Anglias, draped across vinyl-upholstered back-seats, barely hearing the bleat of night-trekking mountain sheep as they went about their business. There was less to be scared about in those days. People didn't even lock their back-doors back then, did they?

The doctor sighed, unscrewed his thermos, poured steamy tea into a cracked plastic cup. He could afford a new one, but wouldn't get the same taste, he told Zina whose wry laughter tinkled gaily through the cupboard-like rooms of their tiny terraced house. The doctor and his wife had never changed home since they had first arrived from London, living always down there in the valley where he had built up his practice so diligently, year by year. If they looked out of their bedroom window, past a line of pea-sticks and cloches, they saw and heard the river. It was enough, in the end, even when they got restless. For her, for him, for their children. Everything was right, wasn't it, as it should be?

As if this brought up something as deep and ancient as the darkness of the hidden mine-workings, Geraint Morris turned East to look for Ivy Cottage, where Arthur and Violet had lived, those people who changed his life so much. Could you see the house? Almost! There were the beech trees, still standing after all the years. You could almost hear the hiss of them, except that he was two miles off and knew better. He wanted to see a smear of blue twisting up which would be smoke from Arthur's living-room fire – but he knew better about that too. It was all long gone; and no doubt the people that mattered were better for that, and at peace.

A distant clatter announced the passing of the Valleys Clipper from Cardiff. As Dr Morris followed the bright carriages trundling up the valley floor, he suddenly saw them clear as crystal in his mind's eye. Arthur and Vi. Arm in arm on the swing-seat in Ivy Cottage garden. It was a fantasy, of course, for that particular couple were never like that, in his time, at least.

– No-one stays that innocent, do they now?

His words sounded odd in amongst the damp, still trees. Dr Morris looked round, embarrassed despite himself. Who on earth would be listening in a place like this! He was probably the only person out for miles around, on this, a grim Sunday morning, with the Church Service hardly over on Radio Four and most souls still packed under their duvets. But it was true, he thought, with a local doctor's wealth of experience. Few people keep their little Eden for long, with all that pain and anger and envy and jealousy and disillusion and the rest which comes and cuts you down to size.

Dr Morris smiled thinly. Faint ploppings around him, told him another autumn shower was on its way. He mustn't stay long, for Zina might already have his cooked Sunday breakfast waiting on the table. Yet still Dr Morris stood hesitant. He gazed again towards those distant beech trees, raising himself an inch or two on tip-toe.

Yes! He could see Ivy Cottage roof. And was that dark blob one half of Arthur and Violet's bedroom window? Dr Morris's eyes watered with the effort and the cold. Damn! He'd tipped his tea over his coat. The doctor gulped the remainder hastily. Tepid, by now, but that was better than nothing.

His way back lay through the perpetual darkness of the Forestry Commission plantation which had long replaced the vivid mysteries of Penlan's old, deciduous woodland. Geraint Morris stopped suddenly. For a moment he just stood there, listening to the far-off murmur of Penlan stream. Then his body stiffened. Was that a voice? It seemed to come from the very depths of the trees. But maybe it was just one those humanish noises sheep sometimes make. Yes, that was it. The man stepped forward briskly. It was then, just at that precise moment as the doctor was fumbling with a recalcitrant collar button, when he suddenly and inexplicably caught the whiff of coarse Navy Cut tobacco, thick and heady in his lungs.

The man bent low. He wanted to be sick. Oh, God. Michael. Why in God's name had he forgotten him? Their son. Arthur and Violet's only surviving child. You wanted to forget, but you never could – quite. And it was hardly surprising, today, that the boy had come back in all his glory. Wasn't it precisely because of him that the police had built that stupid breeze-block wall? The doctor straightened himself up at last. The stench was gone, thank God, yet another ridiculous fantasy. Yet the question came back to the doctor, as always. Was he the one? Did Michael really do it? The police never placed formal charges, of course, but was that why the poor boy had to go and die?

Rain was coming hard, now, even getting down between thousands of invisible pine-needles. Dr Morris got his collar-button done at last, made hurriedly for the main road and home.

# *Condemned*

> *The First Station. Jesus is condemned.*
> *"My loving Jesus, it was not Pilate;*
> *No, it was my Sins that condemned Thee to die . . ."*

Geraint Morris knew little of Arthur's family roots. If he had, a sensitive and intelligent man, he would have made his own connections.

Michael's father was born in 1901, just as an old and diminutive Queen Victoria was laid to rest. Arthur's five elder brothers had taken their names from a string of obscure Old Testament prophets. But he was last in the line and his parents were running out of ideas. At all events, his name sprang from a native source, and a hero not quite so ancient.

Slender, asthenic, young Arthur peered eagerly through a pair of thick pebble lenses from the age of twelve. Later came various strange additions. Pendulous globes of solder, confused strands of gleaming copper wire, later in the thirties, yellowing strips of sticky-backed Boots tape, right across the right hand lens. Arthur was always a man of invention.

One cold November's day, in Penclydach town-centre, pausing for a moment in the course of a shopping errand at a tilted street-corner – young Arthur looked up by chance to see a winter sun suddenly bursting through oceans of unfathomable grey. It was like some mighty transfiguration above the small South-Welsh mining-community. Nobody seemed to be taking the slightest notice, but Arthur's scabby kneecaps shook and his eyes filled with tears behind their lenses. Was all this happening just for him?

Another time, a year or so later, Arthur was running across a field of sodden thistles when he suddenly fell on his face and felt the cold black earth oozing into all the hollows of his body. He had been fishing for sticklebacks. And now a score of silver shapes from his jar writhed uselessly in the tall stems of grass. Arthur found himself briefly considering in a childhood way whether his own short life was so very different from theirs. Maybe there was no need to get back up now. Maybe it would be better to save himself and his parents further trouble by lying here forever. But his father's whisky-soaked cry from the pit-head yard soon put an end to such wild ideas. Arthur pulled himself clumsily up, adjusted his spectacles which now produced weird smudges of black through all things, and trudged manfully homeward. Part of him was, through this and other things, a man.

Arthur fell in love with Violaceae some six years later, quite by chance. They had clambered up to the municipal park, three of them, elder sisters, pushing an ungainly pram which contained the youngest of the brood – baby-brother Timothy. Vi was the oldest and tallest and most pretty. Her full name came from the sweet violet which hugged woodland shades when summer was coming, as Arthur later learned. All Arthur understood on that day in the late spring of 1917, whilst hundreds of miles away soldiers' limbs flew through dank mists of the Somme – was the power of those dazzling lapis lazuli eyes which turned his way so innocuously yet seemed to enter into the very heart . . .
 – Where d'you live then?
 – Over by there.
Her smile, small, dainty. He seemed to rise several inches into the air.
 A week later Arthur and Violet strolled self-consciously into the private wood behind his house to pick the last of the bluebells, already heavy on their stalks, sick with pungency. There in a ferny darkness, their hands finally touched. When they reappeared in the May sunshine, two roses had appeared on Arthur's ascetic cheeks. The front parlour later that afternoon seemed tiny and suffocating as the boy was forced to endure a whole barrage of jibes from his older brothers, black from the coal-face, despite the daily tub.
 – Did you do it, then, did you kiss her?

– Him? Would he ever?
– Tell us, boy, come on now, out with it!

Arthur retreated to the safety of an empty bedroom, listening to roars of laughter down below. Yet as he watched his mug of warm milk shivering between his palms, he found that Vi's eyes and voice had taken over everything. Life could not have offered up a young girl more different. Yet already he yearned for her, body and soul.

In the two years of engagement which followed, Violet returned Arthur's engagement-ring twice with a disdainful smile. Yet at night, in the warmth of a bed shared with her two sisters Lilly and Bridget, she confessed her dreams. They were not that expansive. Born to a family of teachers and book-worms, she was the least intellectual. Her vision of the future went as far as a clean house, a clutch of babies, and the comfort of knowing that her husband had a decent, steady job.

In the latter regard, she judged well. Strange to say, given his nervous disposition, Arthur acquired a professional position at a time when most valley lads were lucky to get promises of work for longer than a week. The reason lay in those two discrete hemispheres which conformed his mind. One side of him wild, errant, poetic . . . the other incorrigibly down-to-earth, brilliant with facts and figures. During weekdays therefore, at the General Post Office telephone-exchange where he worked all his life, the quick-witted, logical side would rule supreme. But then, as dusk came and he returned home to sink into his favourite chair behind some thick volume of philosophy, the other-worldly in him would rise, phoenix-like. Paradoxically, these incongruous polarities remained in perfect equipoise through all the vicissitudes of his later life.

Their wedding, like many in the early twenties, was cheap and practical. The ceremony quickly over, the couple raced down the hill to the railway-station in a veil of driving Welsh rain. Vi's skirts were soaked to the knees by the time they flopped into their third-class seats – but they were happy. Married life had begun in a certain style.

Their marriage was a success at first, but babies refused to come. Many times Violet shed a quiet tear as she travelled the slow-stopping steam-train back up to the mining valleys and her sisters.

Though not religious, she would kneel down in the quiet of the chapel at the bottom of Ash Street, praying for fertility. Finally, three years after that rainy marriage morning, a son was born, miraculously, on Christmas Day, 1929. They called him Michael. Violaceae's eyes shone out their blue. Remembering that moment of transfiguration on a tilted street corner, Arthur's lenses misted over with passion. Deep down, a vision was being born.

A year later, Arthur got promotion. They moved from South Wales, to live in the Midlands. Neither had spent more than a day and a night in England before. It was a tug on their hearts to enter this strange, muted landscape, far from the slate-and-stone terraces which jostled for space above a fast-flowing Clydach stream. But Arthur's practical side was in its ascendancy; and Violet was by nature adaptable. They rented a modest redbrick house beyond the town and made it as comfortable as it was possible for a middle-income family at the start of the thirties. As if in reward for domestic heroisms, a second child was born within a twelve-month. A girl, this time. They called her Anne, the simplest name they could think of, to escape past exoticisms. When Violet came home to Wales to visit her sisters, her voice trembled with a joy they had never noticed before.

1935. Michael was six years old. In a darker world beyond the redbrick suburb, Benito Mussolini invaded Abyssinia. But in England, it was the Silver Jubilee and one bright Spring morning, Arthur and Vi decided to hold their very first children's party. Balloons and crepe-paper trailed across the front-room in a dazzle, all but obliterating Arthur's shelves of philosophy. By mid-afternoon a chatter of strange young voices had invaded the house. At the last moment Arthur took fright at all the new, cheeky faces and retreated to a vegetable patch outside with rake and spade. Violet smiled appeasingly.

– Let him go, love his heart!

She was in her element.

Just before four she popped upstairs to dainty herself up for the arrival of the last of the mothers. As she was crossing the landing she heard a high voice piping up from the hall. It was Annie, announcing that she was going outside with Bella to take a look at her new doll. Busying herself at the dressing-table with face-cream and powder-puff, Violet paused for thought. Where was it that little Bella lived? Across the main road? But Arthur was out there in the garden, wasn't he, poking amongst the pea-sticks? He'd make sure that Annie didn't do anything silly! But Violet had forgotten about her husband's poor eyesight behind those thick spectacles, lenses made filthy from his labours. A scream of brakes through the window changed all that.

She must have blundered downstairs and raced out to the front, although she never remembered. Instead, Violaceae came to, a semblance of herself, shuddering over a tiny human form, twisted and unrecognisable on the smooth tarmac. Neighbours were screaming in a far-away world outside of her. Arthur was there too, in some other cosmos, howling like a dog. But all this meant nothing. Violaceae wept no tears that day, nor any other come to that.

She told no-one the funeral day, not even her sisters. When they met her on Penclydach station several weeks later they didn't even recognise her on the platform. All the usual features were there, but in a new and disturbing arrangement, which was not Violaceae at all.

Arthur was different. He knew how to weep just as he did on that childhood day in Penclydach when the sky opened like a flower. And he still had his first-born and favourite, six-year-old Michael, born so portentously on Christmas Day. Anne's death stabbed deep – but it did not strike his soul dead. Perhaps this was why Violet began to hate her husband. Or perhaps it was because she blamed him for not racing out in time to save poor Annie from the lorry's wheels. At the mundane surface of things, life did not change dramatically, once the unreal rituals of a child's funeral were over. However all trust and feeling was gone between them. Violet turned inward, pale and silent. Arthur turned to his son.

What then of Michael?

There were no photographs taken in these early years, but those taken later on revealed a tall, clumsily-proportioned young man, with a surprisingly winsome delicacy of face. The soft lapis lazuli eyes were clearly his mother's, but the huge, pendulous ears came from the father's side. Michael's full, passionate lips might have come from either, but the tender smile on them must have been young Violaceae's, for Arthur seemed so very serious all his life – even when he wasn't. Finally, that quizzical slant of the eyebrows, like some perpetual question-mark about life, nature, destiny – that belonged to neither parents. It was Michael's own device.

When Annie was taken so inexplicably, Michael was snapped in two. His young sister's nature, eager, decisive, revealed a brave faith in life. Was it such a conviction which took her racing out into the road on that fatal day? By then she had marked her place in the house. Hero-worshipped by her brother, she decided on all the games – and the rules which would apply. Annie led, Michael, the older brother, followed. Like his mother, the boy could not weep after the accident. But at night, clinging to a muddle of bedclothes, he made dull, animal noises. That space, that utter nothingness! Michael was too young to know what to do more than clutch at the unruly blankets and feel his warm urine, comforting, seeping all about.

A year later, Arthur and Violet returned to Wales with a thin, sallow boy twisting at their heels. Arthur had been promoted by the GPO yet again. He drove about the place now in a large black Morris, searching for the perfect home which would bring back something like peace to his family. Miracle of miracles, he found it one day, quite by chance. The name on the white-painted wicket-gate was Ivy Cottage.

Whenever Arthur looked back in later years, he saw first the beech-trees, ranged so majestically around the house. Yet it was not simply the sight of these, but rather their sound and movement which would haunt an old man's fond imagination. The slightest breath of wind would sent a great turbulence through their branches, producing a reverberant hiss which dizzied the mind. In winter, icy gales would make the bare trunks crack and roar through the night, until the sound and fury of it all travelled right inside the soul.

The continental shutters came next in Arthur's later recollections. Sky-blue, gloss-painted, perfectly unorthodox in rural Wales – and ludicrously out of place with the rest of the house. Why had they been put there? An architect's whimsy, it would seem, certainly there was no sensible purpose. For, instead of warm summer sunshine, it was a raw westerly which invariably raced up the smoothness of the glacial valley to hit the house smack in the face on most days of the calendar. Not surprisingly, the shutters remained open throughout the year, offering decoration rather than practical benefit – and were never used against the heat of the sun.

Finally, Arthur would recall the garden with its neat stone-paved paths, dividing flowers and vegetables and grass into neat rectangles. Yet although he was skilful with spade and fork and trowel, it was not Arthur's work which kept this place in order over the years. No, it was Vi, her unrelenting purpose and method. The less she talked, the more she pottered silently outside, with Michael, weed-basket in hand, following assiduously behind. Michael had no green fingers, yet was always eager to offer a helping hand. For unknown to his parents, the garden had become a place of solace, a quiet, insect-humming retreat, away from the complexities of the world.

Inside Ivy Cottage, the rooms were smaller and darker than a visitor might expect. Here, a shuffling of feet, or nervous clearing of throat rarely went unnoticed. It was hard to feel truly alone. Michael's bedroom, unlike his parents, faced north. Counting each of the cottage's fourteen worn stairs as always, Michael would enter his little kingdom and stand beside a small sash-window, gazing out past a confusion of deciduous woodland towards that shape etched sharp against the northern sky, which was Penlan hill. On bitter January mornings, with colours drained and outlines icy-clear, Penlan seemed to stride right up to the house – and press against Michael's thin pane. Sometimes the seven-year-old would open his eyes from sleep and see the dark crags come alive, like giant claws. Still bleared with dreams, Michael witnessed for a brief instant a huge Neolithic beast shifting, stretching, making ready to pounce.

Downstairs, meantime, Arthur sat at an oilcloth-covered kitchen table, cramming Navy Cut tobacco into the first briar pipe of the day. Violaceae would appear from the scullery, setting before her husband a stained mug filled with dark Hornimans tea. The clink of china and spoon, scrape of chair-leg, pad of slippered foot – these were all the communications that appeared left to connect the couple, beyond the sad legacy of the past. It had been love, not friendship which had first connected them – but it was friendship they badly needed now. And so, when their eyes met occasionally by chance across the kitchen table, both quickly looked away.

Then one evening in early June, just a few months after their arrival at Ivy Cottage, Violaceae made a surprising discovery. Weeding around what she thought was just an old lump of Penlan sandstone, her trowel made a noise which sounded weirdly like an echo. Crouching low and laying one ear next to the cold rock, she knocked at the pitted surface a second time and listened to a tapping sound which seemed to go on and on, descending right down into H.G. Wells' Centre of the Earth. Vi sat very still, deep in thought. Her eyes were as dull and lifeless as they had been in a while, but there was now a certain intentness in them, dusk falling imperceptibly all around.

Footsteps, suddenly tripping up, eagerly. A bright-eyed boy, clumsily made, gangling, rubbing one stick-like leg against the other. Vi turned, saw without surprise that her son's lips were decorated with dribbles of orange cordial from the bottle on the kitchen-sill.

– Well, what is it this time?
– Nothing, only –
– Only what?
– You looked funny, and –
– Funny! What d'you mean, you silly thing?

Michael grinned up at his mother, cock-eyed, restless, apologetic. Violet sighed, gave up her catechism, looked back at that lump of strange-sounding stone. What was it?

– Go on, now, Michael dear, fetch your dad.

Michael toddled off, shouting aimlessly for his father. Dusk was spreading a quiet shroud across the sky. An old, hoarse crow called out three times to his mate from the highest of the beech branches. Down in the valley, a line of tiny coal-trucks was crawling back up to the mines. Early gnats whirled about Vi's damp forehead. She flicked at them irritably. The echo of the trowel was still strong in her head, so other-worldly in this place. Suddenly, and with the intensity of an Old Testament vision, she glimpsed a black tunnel crashing its way at a hundred-miles-an-hour, down, down to the heart of everything.

Coughs and clouds of tobacco-smoke, stumbling up. Arthur was finally there standing beside her.

– What is it, love?

Violaceae pointed to her discovery, with a few desultory mutterings. Arthur knelt low, fingering the earth with yellow, picked-down nails.

– Funny, I thought I'd dug all round here.

– Well, you hadn't, had you?

– No. Right. I'll go find a spade, now, shall I love?

– Just do it! Don't go always asking!

So Arthur nodded, lumbered hurriedly off through the gathering darkness, in the direction of the garden-shed. On a nearby peninsular of paving-stone, Michael watched his father's journey dumbly. Vi shrugged to herself, joined her son on the path, absent-mindedly buttoning up his coat. Night was creeping closer. The old crow had flapped off to the other side of Penlan wood. A tiny bat, membraned-wings whirling in a dream of flight – weaved above their heads. Somebody was whistling down in the lane, a traditional air which suddenly made Violet remember a night long ago when dada had talked to his eight little daughters about the Great War.

*The night winds are sighing, the last hour is fled.*

Were those the words? But Arthur was back, with three odd-sized spades propped over one shambling shoulder.

– I thought I'd bring them all, you know, just in case.

Violet laughed dryly. Michael trotted energetically across the damp earth to join his father, jabbing now at the ground with one of the smaller blades. The woman folded her arms, watched them both disappearing into a nebulous black.

– It's too late now. Start again in the morning.

– It won't take long, Vi, you'll see! Just need to make a –

With this, the man threw aside his implement, bent low, began to heave with ludicrous optimism at that implacable weight of Penlan sandstone. Whole minutes passed. Violet's impatience grew, drawing her bottle-green cardigan tight around her shoulders, against the chill of an early-summer night. When would the man ever learn?

As if in answer to her silent interrogation, a slow miracle, as the stone began to rise inch by inch out of the earth. A whoop of joy from the seven-year-old. Violet found herself scampering eagerly towards the spot.

– Wait! Wait for me!

Together, man and wife and child saw the stone finally rolled back. All three gazed down into a blackness that was deeper and more real than the approaching night. Arthur's fingers held his son's tight, just in case. But the boy, possessed of divine inspiration, retrieved a small pebble from the ground and tossed it into the inky space. Moments passed. Then, a faint splashing. Arthur and Violaceae looked at each other, smiled oddly.

They had found Ivy Cottage's well.

In a few short days, Arthur, ever the inventor, had improvised a simple winding-gear, together with mortared wall, coping and slated roof to protect against the elements. On a bright, windswept Saturday afternoon a week later, the moment of truth arrived. Violet had gone into town and bought a coil of builders' rope. Arthur attached an enamel pail and began to lower it down. A louder splash than on that first day told them that it had finally arrived. Michael cried out:

– Let me! Let me!

So it was the little boy who began to winch the bucket back up, heavy with its burden. As it reached the top, Arthur lent a hand. A squeal of triumph. The pail bobbed into the day's hissing sunshine. Lapping within it, the clearest water you could imagine. Violet dipped her fingers in and discovered it was also the coldest water in all the world.

They returned to the cottage with their precious discovery. The pail lay on the kitchen table, however, for a whole half-hour, as a furious argument ensued between Arthur and his wife, as to whether it was hygienic to use water from a disused well for making tea. Finally Violaceae won a compromise, Arthur promising to boil the water a whole ten minutes before it met the brew. The task was duly done, Michael, watching excitedly. Then, a pregnant pause. All sat, lifted their brimming cups, drank silently. Yes. They agreed it was the best cup of tea they had ever tasted.

Something altered at Ivy Cottage on that breezy Saturday. When Arthur and Violent went to bed that night they found themselves clinging awkwardly at the top of the stairs. It was not something they had done for a while. Tears rose in the woman's eyes, but did not fall. Not quite . . .

Things were different for young Michael too. Now, most days, he would wander down to the well, sit on the coping for five minutes or more, staring solemnly down. One afternoon his father wandered up, sat down beside him. Arthur noticed an intentness in his son which he hadn't seen before.

– What is it, boy?
– Her.
– Who?

Michael looked up at his father with those gentle, lapis lazuli eyes and Arthur felt a sudden prickle of fear.

Both stared down into the blackness. A breeze rose up from somewhere down the valley and took possession of the trees. For a brief moment the air was filled with the hissing of a thousand beech-branches – and there was the giddy smell of sap and bark.

– Did you say something, boy?
– No, dad.
– Funny. I must be dreaming.

Was it her or just the wind? Neither dared to utter the word Annie, which had been banished from the family vocabulary since the day when that ridiculously small coffin bobbed finally out of view. The breeze dropped as suddenly as it had come. Father and son rose, returned to the house, where Violet was busy with dinner. Arthur sat in front of the fire and for no reason he could fathom opened a dusty volume from a nearby shelf, to find a page marked with a scrap of yellowing newspaper, murmuring the first words that came to his eye.

*A soul cannot live apart from God,*
*nor the body apart from the soul.*

Later that night, crouched next to Violaceae's slack arms, the man dreamt of his daughter for the first time in many months. Pure, untouched, without a single blood-stain. Outside, meanwhile, somewhere in the dark South-Welsh earth, water was trickling between shelves of ancient Penlan rock, onward, endlessly replenishing.

# *Bearing*

> *The Second Station. Our Lord receives the Cross.*
> *"Beloved Jesus, I embrace all Tribulations*
> *Thou hast destined for me until Death . . ."*

Beyond Ivy Cottage, and the three people who lived within in it, lay the wood. It was a mysterious place in those far-off pre-war days when Geraint Morris was still a child – before geometric pine-trunks arrived to claim the land. Yet it was not quite wilderness, even then. For beneath leaf and fern and moss lay the signs of men. Primitive iron-ore smelting had once, generations earlier, been a feature of this place, filling the glades with the smell of charcoal and pony sweat. Now heaps of weirdly-shaped pumice were all that remained to mark the site of the furnaces. Further north across the valley, the curious traveller might find odd-shaped ditches and mounds, evidence of the many labyrinthine tunnels gouged out by miners of old. But you had to know what you were looking for. Nothing looked now as it once was. All had been altered by time.

One day, walking alone as usual with hazel stick and smoking briar, Arthur noticed a faint gleam in the woodland gloom. He stopped, knelt down to feel the shocking smoothness of an old tramway rail, hardly rusted despite the years. Rising to his feet, he gazed through a maze of feather-like birch-branches to see how the tram's path marked a ruler-line across the woodland floor, which even now, years on, could not be quite erased.

Arthur was a strong walker, but it took him a long time to plumb all the wood's secrets – if he ever did. The wide bridle-paths tell a man little. But if you take the risk and dive into a narrow forest track, the chances are that it will peter out after fifty yards or so, and, if you do not immediately retrace your steps, you will soon be quite lost. In such ways Penlan wood kept hold of its mysteries, despite the foragings of men. For his part, Arthur was not unduly sad, for deep down he loved things best that could not be quite explained. Or at least one hemisphere of him did – far from the GPO Exchange.

Violet, despite her name, did not like the wood. It frightened her, especially at dusk, when aboriginal terrors seemed to race through the shadowy trunks. Sometimes, armed with a wicker picnic-basket, she might be persuaded to venture out upon some family expedition, perhaps with one of her sisters to lend moral support. But in general she preferred the order and symmetry of the house. One day, tempted into an autumn glade by her husband in search of blackberries, she thought she glimpsed a bright-eyed face gazing impishly at her from behind a gnarled oak. She fled through the autumn twilight, leaving a trail of echoey screams. From that time forth, the idea of some woodland sprite, clad in the winsome shape of her daughter, was enough to set her implacably against anything that lay beyond the lamp-lit sanity of Ivy Cottage.

And little Michael?

Something in that anxious eight-year-old yearned to creep out of the house in the heart of the night to lie down amongst ferns and mosses for ever. If Annie's elfin spirit did indeed inhabit the oak trunks, then it might have been a further inducement to escape. But there was a difficulty. A darkness now sat behind the boy's eyes, from all that had happened. And even when he sat beside the well-head, aboard the gently-swinging garden-seat which his father had so ingeniously fashioned – even then Michael could not overcome his disquiet. And so, like his mother, the boy kept his distance from Penlan wood. The wood meant dreams – and dreams, for quite different reasons, were dangerous to them both.

Thus Arthur ventured forth alone, wending his way through the dappled glades on a sunny Saturday morning all the way up to Penlan's craggy summit. Here, a thousand feet up, he would stagger, gasp at the icy air, and survey, God-like, every side of that many-faceted glacial valley which was his home.

Below, the Welsh slopes spoke to him. They were never silent, even at dead of night. Slow shunters, beetle-like motor-cars, the iron-foundry, the steam-powered mine-ventilator, the cry of man and beast – all these sang out in unholy chorus, without cease. And the shape of the steep scarps, like some vast loudspeaker, amplified each fragment of sound, so that Arthur could sit there on a cold lip of Penlan rock and fancy he could not just see but also hear into the heart of all things.

Far below in his bedroom, Michael stood nose pressed against the window pane, saw a familiar matchstick-shape up there on the crag – and waved for all he was worth. But Arthur, behind those pebble lenses clouded by sweat and dirt, saw nothing.

Summer finally came in that year of 1938. At Lilly and Bridget's firm instigation, the family took a proper holiday for the very first time. Young Michael had never seen the sea. Awkward-limbed, he strode clownishly across the wet shingle of a Pembrokeshire shoreline, confronted the rough whiteness of storm-tide waves, heard a roar that seemed older than time – and a smile came to his lips which was new. Arthur glimpsed the moment, yards away, sitting upon a hammock-like shelf in the windy dunes. Beside him, a stolid heaviness on the plaid car-rug. Arthur looked across at his wife. Has she noticed? But no, Violet had missed her son's transcendent smile, gazing down at a much-thumbed copy of Good Housekeeping.

*Ten things you can do with cross-stitch*

Days later the sun disappeared and the weather grew grey and heavy. They arrived home on a hot late-August afternoon, the coming storm lying clammily about everything as they entered the house. Michael scampered first into the kitchen – then stopped short. Something horribly new was here, filling his nostrils with ghastly sweetness.

The sickly odour of corrupting flesh.

Close behind her son, Violet gave out a choked moan. Pragmatism to the fore, Arthur stumbled ahead, handkerchief bunched over his face. His senses took him fast to the source. A hunk of raw mutton, left in the cold-store cupboard ten days before. As he stared, the meat seemed to come alive, its pock-marked surface peopled by innumerable maggoty shapes.

– Bloody hell!

Vi rushed furiously past the transfixed form of her husband, pulled on a pair of rubber gloves, speedily disposing of the horrific object beneath a mass of local newspaper from under the kitchen-chair.

– Fool! I told you three times to check the house!

Arthur shrugged, mumbled a few inconsequential excuses – but Vi was already gone, storming out of the cottage, bearing the horrid burden before her, arms stretched out like a pair of sugar tongs.

That same afternoon, Arthur took his largest spade to the back-garden and dug a hole almost up to his waist before Violet would allow him to stop.

– There, now. Right. That will do.

Storm clouds floated heavily above, like basking whales. Nearer, two familiar crows circled uneasily. Closer still, a pestilence of hungry blue-bottles peopled the air as Violet bent low to place a neatly-parcelled offering deep in the dark, coal-streaked earth. Unaccountably Arthur's eyes filled with tears. He wiped them off angrily. Vi must not see! But she was oblivious to everything, shuffling back towards the house, muttering to herself.

– I told him. I told him three times!

Michael had seen his father's tears. Something flickered in the lid of his left eye which would years later be diagnosed:

*Nervous tic. Irregular. Aetiology, unknown.*

For the moment, no-one noticed it, however. Stillness, then a diminutive voice tested the gloom.

– Can I do anything, Dad?

– No, boy. Not, now.

– What if I help cover up?

– What? Oh, yes. The hole. You do that, now, Michael.

And so it was that Arthur left his young son, ineffectually transferring scraps of Penlan earth back into the mutton-joint's grave as he wandered after his wife into the house. How that meat stank still! How long would this terrible sweetness remain? Arthur met Violaceae's sullen eye in an unlit kitchen. The man nodded as if in answer to some obscure philosophical question – before stumbling past towards the angle of the stairs. Moments later, in the seclusion of his bedroom, Arthur composed his hands on his lap and let all those tears fall free.

A couple of months after this event, Violet developed an unlikely passion which would change her life. It began one afternoon in late October when by chance she paused in front of Mr Champion's newsagent's shop in the village square, and saw something new in its window-display. The woman gazed, sauntered casually inside, began chattering to Mr Champion about Spain and the Anti-Comintern Pact and other high-sounding matters. But all the while her beady eye was on that small packet in the window which she finally secured for a few coppers, and dropped lightly into her shopping-basket.

Walking home along a lane already pitted by Autumn torrents, Violet could not help but stop in her tracks, delving into her bag to examine her prize. The cardboard container was grey, nondescript, but when you tore it open things changed. How they shimmered in her hands, those royal suits, as she fanned them in the twilit road! Now, was the King the highest, or the Queen? And what about that arrogant, mustachioed Knave? Violaceae scoured the past for clues and for a brief moment something of that first young dream of happiness flickered in her lapis lazuli eyes. Her face grew ten years younger, recalling a pretty teenager jumping up and down on a tilted Penclydach pavement, screaming out for another stab at hopscotch.

– My go!

– No, mine! Me!

The moment went almost as soon as it had come. But as Vi resumed her walk home there was a perceptible change in her stride. She arrived to an empty house. Michael was still at school. Seating herself comfortably in Ivy Cottage's small front-parlour (used only on Sundays, or for guests), the woman spread out neat rows of cards for Patience on the floor. She dealt herself the first card with trembling fingers. Ace of Clubs! A thrill went through her and time made a Einsteinian leap so that when she next looked up it was night and she had been crouched over her game for two hours at least.

Back home from the Telephone Exchange, loosening his company-tie in the low cottage doorway, Arthur stared curiously at his wife, hunched there over the carpet, amidst a litter of diamonds and spades. Hearing her husband's polite cough, Vi rose guiltily.

– I made dumplings. Only take a moment! Just need to warm them up –

She hurried past into the kitchen, dropping a two-of-hearts next to Arthur's left shoe. Arthur bent, picked up the card.

– What's this, then, love?
– What d'you think?
– Never knew you played.
– Well, now you do!

Next evening father and son watched unseen and incredulous as Violet sat at her small sewing-table – now covered in cheap curtain baize – muttering divers instructions to herself as she dealt four hands for gin-rummy. Arthur made a quiet sign to his son. The pair tip-toed back to the kitchen. There, the man prepared a pot of tea in his usual absent-minded fashion, tipping well-water and milk and sugar in equal proportions.

– Never knew she liked it. Did she ever say to you?

Michael solemnly shook his head.

– Maybe she'd like us to join in. Play along with her. What d'you think, then, eh, boy?

Michael shrugged vaguely.

– No. Right, then. Best to leave her to it. What d'you say?

The tea was steeped and duly poured. Arthur sat heavily beside his son, took up a cracked saucer and began to ladle out measures of thick brown liquid, blowing raspingly across its turbid surface, before he noisily sipped. As always, Michael watched, horribly entranced. As always Arthur pointed at his son's cup with playful admonition.

– Don't let it go cold, now, boy!

Michael ladled out a diminutive proportion. Father and son sipped at their saucers, measure for measure, deep in thought. Then something strange happened. A peal of girlish laughter, echoing ghost-like through the passages of the tiny house. Arthur and Michael stared at each other, astonished.

Vi had not laughed like that in all of remembered time.

Six months later Violet joined the local whist-drive. Thereafter, each Wednesday night for twenty years, she would button her coat to the neck before hurrying up the mountain road to that low Nissen hut which served as a village hall, joining a garrulous female company for the rituals of the game. She never laughed girlishly again, as she did that day at Ivy Cottage. But somehow her instinct for the game made her popular all the same. When Christmas came around she made three yeast cakes for the annual party. The following year she ran the raffle (All Proceeds to War Amputees). Eight years on, she was voted Chairman. For such a silent, weighed-down woman, this was no mean achievement. At home, meanwhile, Arthur thumbed lovingly through his latest purchase from the Left Book Club and felt his heart a little easier.

Is she happier? Yes. Just a bit.

Christmas Day, 1938. Michael's ninth birthday. As if in answer to Arthur's prayer, snow lay thick on the ground and the boy's face broke into a wide grin. His father bustled at the kitchen table, unpacking onto the oilcloth a balsa-wood kit for Kingsford Smith's famous tri-motor Fokker which first flew across the Atlantic ten years before. Armed with tracing-paper, razor-blades and a tub of glue, father and son toiled all the way to Boxing-Day. Finally, their Great Work was complete.

– What d'you think, then?

Michael's eyes flashed out in the dark.

Next day, Arthur stood on Ivy Cottage lawn, winding propeller-elastic a full hundred strokes, before tilting the Fokker's frail fuselage into the wind.

– Ready, Michael?

Michael nodded. Arthur drew breath, and with a surprisingly delicate motion of his arm sent the plane into the air. Yes! There it went, arching through a pale winter sunlight. Michael's face grew still with wonder. How it buzzed and gleamed and looped the loop! Then, just as suddenly, its journey was ended by a beech branch and the Fokker became just a jumble of crumpled shapes, swaying in the wind. Arthur's longest bean-stick finally got it down. But now there was an ugly tear where Kingsford Smith had once waved to the press photographers, beyond all repair.

– Never mind, eh? Always make another.

Spring came. The woods began to look different. The beech trees made new sounds. One bracing March morning, Arthur persuaded his son to walk with him as far as Penlan stream. A family of magpies squawked promiscuously from blossoming thorn-tree branches as they arrived next to the torrent. For a while they made dams and raced twig-boats absorbedly, children together in restless dapples of sun. Arthur finally paused, lenses smeared with clay. In his nostrils the sulphurous odour of mud. At his feet, the glint of early celandines. In his ears the cry of an excited nine-year-old. Happiness hit like a hammer-blow. Why! What about poor Annie? Happiness went on, fierce, triumphant. Arthur let go, then, as the celandines flamed inside. Why fight? Why turn always away?

*This is my son. See? There he is*

Later that same morning, as they scrambled through Penlan's thickets high above the stream, kicking up clouds of last year's leaves – Michael suddenly stopped short, stared and pointed.

– What's that, dad?

A strange darkness, looming a few yards away, between slender trunks of birch. What was it? Arthur's eyes blinked behind their lenses. He strode quickly forward, stopping before a wedge of pale, weather-smoothed limestone. There, at his feet, an opening no bigger than an eleven-year-old. The man bent low, felt a breath of icy air come up from far away. Why had he missed this in all his wanderings? Michael's light footsteps, suddenly scampering up through dry leaves, breaking into his puzzled thoughts.

– Dad?

– Yes, Michael?

– Is it deep, then?

– Yes, it's deep.

Somewhere far off came the clack-clack-clack of a shunter braking on some downward incline from the coalfields. Then the sad mewing of a buzzard. Then just the leaves, rustling under their feet.

– As deep as our well?

– Who knows? Maybe. Maybe deeper.

Michael took a while to take that in. Arthur thought of the day when he missed the sound of that approaching lorry – and put a protective hand on his son's shoulder, just in case. The lad looked up at his father, disappointed.

– Can't we try?

– No – not today.

– When?

– Later. When you're older, mmm?

They turned, sauntered back down to the brook. A redbreast was singing now, where speckles of blue interspersed the yellow-green budding of spring. Something about the boy's tight fingers in his told Arthur that there was another question coming.

– Well, son? What is it?

– Nothing only –

– I know you – out with it!

Michael's lapis lazuli eyes seemed to gaze through him.

– What d'you call people who explore caves and that – ?

Arthur picked up a piece of iron-ore pumice, fingered it curiously, lobbed it noisily into a dune of dry leaves.

– Geologists. They're called geologists.

– Can I be one?

Arthur stared down at his child in surprise. The boy's face had a stillness which touched him.

– You'll have to work hard.

– I will! I will!

Michael tumbled joyously down the scarp, scattering leaves in a golden mist, leaving his father to the twilight and the song of the redbreast. Next day, they sat at the kitchen table and made a list of tasks. First they would visit the municipal library and borrow a good textbook on the subject, next they would travel the woods and collect every kind of stone they could find, finally they would identify and label each of their discoveries.

– Will we find gold, dad?

– I really don't think –

– Bet you we do!

Michael's bedroom started to change. Old shoe-boxes began to appear, lining the shelves. Inside each one, swathed in cotton wool, lay fragments of different coloured stone, taken from Penlan and beyond. Each piece bore its neat gummed label, covered in spidery latin, etched by the nine-year-old with indelible Indian Ink. Watching his son at work, Arthur felt a glow of pride. Could it be that they were fighting off the past? At his side suddenly, Violaceae, pressing her hand on the hollow between his shoulders. She had not done that for five years. Was the spell finally broken, he thought wildly. Was it?

A few months later war came a second time to the lives of the couple. Arthur's age, together with the nature of his work at the telephone exchange, ensured that he would never be called up for active service. Violet smiled thinly at the news and for one horrid moment Arthur wondered if she was sorry he wasn't going to leave her and be conveniently killed on some faraway field. Quelling the thought he packed more stale tobacco into his pipe, took a spill from the mantelpiece, lit it in the kitchen fire.

Christmas, 1939. Michael's tenth birthday. Rationing made it a simpler affair than last year, yet Arthur still wanted to do his son proud. And so the man saved three-pence a week from his wages to buy a second-hand microscope, complete with its set of lenses and specimen-slides. Violet polished up all the faded brass surfaces through Christmas-Eve night so that by next morning the boy stared at a gleaming wonder, set on the pitted oilcloth of the kitchen table.

– What shall we look at?

Father and son spent that same afternoon turning tiny grains of Penlan stone into boulders and dead flies from the windowsill into towering dinosaurs. There was a quiet purpose about the boy which made both parents pause. That evening, listening to a patter of Welsh rain from the comfort of their bed, Arthur and Violet found themselves suddenly chattering compulsively.

– D'you think he's more settled, do you?

– There you go with your stupidness?

– The boy's changed. You must see that!

– Maybe.

Violet's face made the semblance of a concession in the twilit room. The downstairs clock chimed midnight. They both listened, heard a familiar rustling as their son turned in his sleep.

– Just a little.

Arthur put out the light. They cuddled in the dark. Arthur found himself running his fingers through his wife's permed hair.

– And are you happier, now, Vi? Mmm?

He felt her shrug, through the bedclothes. It was the tiniest of acknowledgements, but even so a small current went through Arthur and he saw for the first time in a while, in a rush of bluebells, a teenage girl offering the smoothness of her cheek for his kisses.

Next day, early, Michael tiptoed excitedly downstairs to try out another speck of Penlan stone under the lens. Some obscure impulse made him halt there, toes tingling with the cold of the hallway tiles. It was something about the silence of the house and the unseen beech trees beyond. Michael hesitated, stepped forward, lifted the door-latch.

Early morning sunshine lunged into the house, flinging sparks of yellow into his young eyes. He felt his whole body stiffen, as if ship's chains held him. And through a veil of rising tears he seemed to see a flock of bright-winged angels, huddled on the beech branches like a thousand fluffed-out pigeons, waiting patiently just for him. The ten-year-old hurled the door shut, panting, praying for the normality of an Ivy Cottage twilight to return. It did, slowly. Ordinariness came back, as it does. Yet this moment of unexpected vision – like that experienced by his father years before on a tilted Penclydach pavement – Michael never forgot. And even in the dark times that were to come, he would glimpse that flock of bright forms in the beech-trees, in all their finery, flapping and squawking for all they were worth.

# *Falling*

> *The Third Station. Jesus falls for the First Time.*
> *"My Jesus, it is the Weight not of the Cross;*
> *But of my Sins which has made Thee suffer so . . ."*

Geraint Morris was just a month or so too young to join up, when war began, so he watched all his pals troop off to the station with a mixture of envy and relief. Days later, strolling with rod-and-line across a desolate Barry Island sands, the teenager gazed out towards that thin grey strip which was the Bristol Channel and found himself wondering what it would be like to die for King and Country. Already he yearned in his heart of be a saver of lives rather than a destroyer. His father, worried by money and responsibility, wanted him to stay home and go into the family business, but Geraint had no brain for a shop-keeper's measures and numbers and knew he had to find a path of his own. His young, fine-boned face already bore witness to will, intelligence and sensitivity – and he had an ally in his mother who wanted to be a nurse when she was his age, so she said. If all went well, in a year or so's time, after the war and everything was over, he would travel up to London and get a proper physician's training. Then in three or four years – who knows? A private consultant, maybe, famed for numerous medical discoveries! Geraint stopped, threw a few ducks-and-drakes. Ripples faded. The sea seemed so still and calm once more. Looking around, he saw how the wide sandy beach went on and on to the horizon. It was if he was the only one left living. An hour later Geraint hooked a large fish but still couldn't shake off the loneliness. That night, lying in bed, he tried to imagine the sound of machine-guns and ack-ack and the shriek of NCOs, but somehow they just wouldn't come. Next morning he made for the call-up office and lied about his age. They sent him back home cheerfully. He wasn't the first to try it:

– Count yourself lucky, Sunny Jim!

Geraint felt shamed all the same. He wanted to get so much out of life. Yet the world didn't seem quite ready for him. When would he get to be a hero like everyone else?

Twenty miles away, Michael's schooldays went by quietly enough on the surface. The village Primary was a low-roofed, red-tiled affair crouched between oblongs of tarmac and tall scotch pine. At the end of each play-time, Mr Morgan, the headmaster, would appear on the front-step, flushed and rotund, waving a hand-bell for all he was worth. A dozen or more grubby village ten-year-olds would tear screaming inside, Michael's ungainly form amongst them. The boy's place was near the back of the class. There, if he craned his neck to his left, he might gaze up at another, steeper scarp of Penlan hill, where rain-clouds scudded dreamily, bringing thick Welsh rain.

Inside, the standard-four classroom was a twilight which smelt of lead-pencils, powder-paint and anxious young sweat. The seat of Michael's desk was glass-like, polished by generations of restless boys and girls. But if he drew his finger across the lid he would encounter a very different Moon-like terrain, where, over time, countless pen-nibs and knife-blades had traced out names. Amongst these, somewhat lighter and more recent, was a single letter carved painstakingly by the desk's latest occupant, using an old pipe-scraper borrowed from his father's desk:

For Anne. Who else?

There had been a time when Michael had played normally with other children. But after his sister's death he found it hard to be open or easy. Instead, wandering uncertainly into the schoolyard, the boy felt their eyes upon him, bayonet-points, poking, finding him out. Michael's persistent introversion became in the end a source of mirth. Away from the care and protection of his parents, the boy was a frail vessel, bobbing on a raging sea. Returning home down a leaf-strewn mountain road after yet another tormented day, Michael felt his heart thud against his chest, loud as the headmaster's cane. Young as he was, he had begun to judge and find himself wanting.

– If only I was like the others!

If only. At such moments Michael felt that life had got the better of him, and he was like one of those sticklebacks his father had told him about, wriggling uselessly in the high Penclydach grass. Yet he was a survivor, like his father, despite everything. He would find a way to get through.

As the youngster crept into the darkness of Ivy Cottage, he saw at the turn in the stair the fixed figure of his mother. Michael's eye caught hers in a sudden nakedness and Violaceae saw the hurt and helplessness all at once. Anger burned through her, yet she said nothing. Like so many mothers before her, she turned to other easier things for comfort, heaping extra portions of ration-book cornedbeef onto her son's dinner-plate, later that night. Heavy-stomached, yet still hungry for love and understanding, the boy trudged up to his bed, counting the fourteen stairs as always, in time to the chimes of the parlour clock.

– One and two and three and four and –

Until he was calm enough to face the dark.

It was about this time that he began to bite his nails to the quick. This, like the small tic under his left eye, would be noted later:

*Anxiety state. Mild. Chronic. Unspecified*

Observing his son over the Daily Chronicle the next morning, Arthur felt a father's pang. The man sucked hard on his over-filled pipe, said nothing. Like his wife, he could not quite find the knack of helping out in such situations, though in his case more from diffidence than from shame. And so a pattern of silence was set in train in Ivy Cottage as the war raged on and Michael grew achingly towards manhood. Returning up the dim incline of the mountain road, towards yet another day of schoolyard torment, Michael felt more and more that he must find a way through on his own.

The boy's dreams grew vivid. One night, a great tangled web covered the entire Penlan landscape, criss-crossed by the feet of gigantic house-spiders. Another night the white-capped Irish Sea he had once seen on a Pembrokeshire coastline came crashing right up to Ivy Cottage's back-door. Another night his small bedroom seemed to turn into a green, foetid swamp . . . Jolting awake in the deep of night, Michael felt sweat prickling at his forehead. Some obscure impulse took him out of bed and across to his bedroom window, where he looked down at the garden, and that farthing-sized piece of thicker darkness, next to the swing-seat, which was the well they had discovered just a few summers ago. Night gusts rattled the window-frames. Beech branches creaked eerily. Then, out of nowhere, a thin whisper, just inches away . . .

– Go on! I dare you!

Suddenly, in a great whoosh, Michael felt himself diving right out through the glass astride a balsa-wood Fokker, down, down, past his father's ingeniously constructed well-head, plummeting on and on, deeper and deeper, to the very Centre of All Things. Seated there, in faery costume, a smiling form.

– Hello, Mikey.
– Hello Anne.
– Don't cry, lovey! Shall we play a game?

Michael felt the feathery lightness of her fingers across his cheeks, there, still standing at his bedroom window as the winds quietly hissed and creaked towards dawn. How alive she was! How achingly tender her voice! No-one else had seen her. Only him. He was the chosen one. This made the gawky boy suddenly godlike and all-powerful.

No-one else shall ever know!

Possessed of a mystic key, Michael felt now that he no longer need bother with those humdrum vicissitudes which had previously perplexed his soul. And so at school next morning, his eyes, oddly dilated, drifted past the grinning children, past the puzzled form-teacher, past crowded blackboard and damp-patches on the wall – on and up to the dazzling blue of the sky above the playground, where, back aboard his Fokker, he frolicked with a spirit-shape amongst noisy trails of larks.

Foraging uncertainly through a grey mound of Violet's mashed-potato that evening, Arthur's eye wandered towards the familiar place where his son sat, humming quietly to himself.

What was it that was different?

– Alright Michael?

Michael dutifully stopped his humming, looked up.

– Mmm? Alright, is it, lad?

The boy nodded slowly, his eyes gazing placidly just past his father towards a point on the kitchen wall where a paintwork crack made the shape of a diminutive Nile. Arthur pursed his lips. What was going on inside Michael's head?

Normality was suddenly back there in the room, with Vi bustling noisily in, dragging behind her the old conked-out Hoover, corpse-like with entrails of tangled electrical flex. She planted the object with decisive fury on the worn stone slabs.

– You promised! Remember?

He did. And so, sprawling the dusty mechanism across a mound of war-strewn newspaper, Arthur bent with screwdriver, copper wire and GPO-issue torch. For the moment, the confusion was gone, drifted off into the ether. But it was back again a week later, filling his pipe as Vi's fingers darted assiduously through her sewing basket.

– Don't you feel it, Vi? He's not like he was. I don't know what it is. Something about his eyes – the way they look past you.

Violet's face, looking up, alert, full of card-sharper's cunning.

– What d'you mean?

– That's the trouble! Can't quite put my finger on it –

Violet surveyed her husband's earnest features, wondering for the thousandth time why it was that she didn't right this second crush those silly pebble-glasses under her shoe. Instead, fingers drumming the side of her sewing basket, her lips fashioned an ironic smile.

– What are you moithering on about now!

– Don't tell me you haven't noticed, love?

– Notice what? Goodness knows! You drive me to distraction sometimes!

– Never mind. It doesn't matter.

Just the ticking of the clock now, and the sound of her husband scouring out his filthy pipe into the fire. Vi's knuckles, pale on her lap, amongst tangles of wool.

– You always do that!

– Do what, Vi?

Violaceae rose, scattering a dozen cotton reels over the carpet, stalked to the door. There she halted, looked back, finally met her husband's eye.

– There's nothing wrong with him, except that he gets spoiled silly by those that should know better.

And with that, she was gone.

Upstairs, Michael sat on his bed, swinging his legs in the dimness in time to those strange mooings and barkings which were, he knew, another Ivy Cottage argument. Somehow he guessed it was about him tonight, but yet it did not bother him as it might have a week or two before – for now Annie was there, an invisible companion, bare feet swinging in time to his.

– Alright Mikey?

– Yeah.

It was the summer of 1941. Michael had discovered that if he scrunched up his eyes really tight and pressed his hands hard against his ears, he could make Annie come as near as the green and gold beech branches hissing outside his window. Even in lessons, when he had to preserve certain appearances, he found that by stretching his hand under the desk as far as it would go, he could feel Annie's fingers touching his, in that magical space he had now constructed – and all the sniggers in all the schoolrooms of the world meant nothing any more.

At about this time Arthur got another promotion. Proud as punch, the new Regional Under-Manager set forth his row of perfectly-sharpened HB pencils across a pine desk which was twice as large as before. Clerks knocked politely upon the frosted-glass. Young secretaries simpered as their feet clicked past him in the long yellow-lamped corridors. Even Violet's stiff face broke into a proud smile as she laid a plate of best ration-book Sunday-dinner at her husband's place at the end of Arthur's first week.

– There love! Just the way you like it!

That was the day Arthur brought his wife home a heart-shaped box of luxury Cadburys chocolates, even though it was two whole weeks before their anniversary. It was time to put tragedy behind. Who knows? Now that Michael seemed to be settling down, and with a little more spending money to bring home, even though the bloody War never seemed to end, maybe they could – just possibly – be a real family again.

A week later, Arthur stopped short before a second-hand-shop window. There, hemmed around by dusty porcelain and pewter, was an enormous Bakelite object, which made the new under-manager's eyes gleam behind his thick lenses. Arthur strode quickly within. A brief debate over the price (Arthur was no barterer), followed by a massing of coins and notes from Arthur's pockets onto the grimy counter, finally the signing of the bill of sale which Arthur folded carefully into his wallet. Next day he returned to the shop in the Morris, hurriedly chucking out a clutter of old newspapers and magazines from the back-seat to make room.

– Goodness gracious, Arthur, what is it?

– A Radiogram!

Violet and Arthur turned to stare open-mouthed at their son, standing there with a smile of triumph in the doorway. They had never been able to afford such things for the house before. So how did young Michael know its name? Arthur shrugged, knelt down on the living-room carpet to start fiddling with wires and switches. Later, with Michael following dutifully, Arthur mounted the stairs uncoiling a reel of fine wire bought specially from the local ironmongers. Living right under the shadow of Penlan hill they would need all the radio-signal they could get. The step-ladder stood ready there on the landing, beneath a small loft trap-door. Arthur hesitated, gave his young son the honour of climbing the ladder, carrying the improvised aerial up to its final attic-home.

Father and son returned to the living room, a mass of nervous anticipation. Violet had entered into the spirit of things, preparing a tray of tea and Nice biscuits. Such was their excitement, the two men took little notice of her offering. The father knelt low at the altar, tremblingly switched on. As valves glowed within its depths, a mysterious hissing and wailing filled the room. Violaceae took a fearful step back, tipping her husband's cup of tea onto the carpet. No-one noticed. Arthur's fingers were now busily twirling the frequency-knob searching vainly amongst a mass of noisy airwaves. Michael's large ears pricked. He gave an excited cry, bounded up, made a grab at the tuner.

– Me, dad! Please!

Arthur studied his son's concentrated features, suddenly so like his baby sister's.

– Please! Go on!

– Alright, then, boy. You try.

Arthur stepped away, gulped what remained in his tea-cup as he watched his son rotating the knob with a child's quick instinct. Did he really know what he was doing? As if in answer, a far-off, storm-tossed Viennese orchestra entered the cottage, playing Johann Strauss's *Voices of Spring*. Violaceae was frozen with wonder. Arthur face's shone.

– I knew he'd do it.

Smiling oddly, Vi nodded. Arthur rose, tousled his son's errant mop of hair and, as if in confirmation of the evening's miracle, a charge of static electricity shot through both child and man.

Michael stood there, hands making little dancing shapes in time to the music. There was no sign now of that shiver next his eye. No. His face was as clear and as calm as it had ever been, for unknown to the world he was watching a tiny, faery shape waltzing to and fro across the stars.

– See, Mikey? See what I can do!

– Yes, Annie. I see.

A week later news came through to the village that young Eddie Watkins had been killed by a single pellet of shrapnel whizzing across the deck of his convoy escort-destroyer. Violet was pegging out whites in the garden when she heard an echo of spiked boots along the village lane. The odd thing was their silence, she thought later. Just those clattering feet, slowly approaching, slowly passing by.

Eddie's mother had been found hanging from the big oak tree in the woods. There was a crumpled note on the acorn-strewn ground, beneath her yellow fingers. Now they were carrying her home, on a farm-door. No-one thought to call on Ivy Cottage. Why should they? Those people were 'quiet sorts'. Later that same afternoon Arthur and Violet went to the old woman's cottage bearing a basket of freshly-cut flowers from the garden for poor William, the Foundryman, who had lost the two people he had loved most in a single week.

They said nothing to Michael, but children have a way of finding out despite our best intentions. That night the boy turned the frequency-knob with infinite care until he found the Andante from Schubert's Unfinished Symphony. The three of them sat and listened, in silence.

The days shortened and Christmas time came round again. As a birthday treat, Arthur and Violaceae took their young son on the slow train, twisting north towards the steep Clydach valley and a huge Christmas-day feast, prepared by the aunts in defiance of all the exigencies of war.

After dinner, Michael was allowed an hour by himself next to the brook which chattered close to the house. There, amongst a litter of old bean-sticks and cabbage stalks, Michael knelt low until he was right next to the icy current and began to race his ash-twigs just like he used to do with his father, at home, years before. After a while, time seemed to go into a loop which took the boy far from who and where he was. God-like, he stooped over the tiny waves, mesmerised by their constantly-changing reflections. And there, all the time amongst the dizzy shapes and colours, was something dark and still which was himself. Michael suddenly wanted to dive there and then into the depths. Perhaps then, everything bad would be put to rest and he might dwell with his sister forever.

– Go on! Do it!

The temptation lasted but a moment – but it was long enough to chill to the quick. He swayed, like some drunkard, eye rolling, glassy. Arthur's footsteps called him back to his senses and to a grey December afternoon. There was a smell of ivy stems and coke-ash and dog-shit which made him want to be sick. His father caught him just before he fell. The man carried him ham-fistedly back to the house.

– What is it? What happened?
– Dunno. Some kind of faint.

They put him on the old couch where Mama used to sit and knit and gossip. Aunt Lilly ran upstairs for smelling salts. Violet sat rubbing her boy's icy fingers.

– Was it a fit or something? Shall we get Doctor Philips?

King George was speaking to the Nation somewhere far off, Michael later remembered, something about bravery and loyalty and sacrifice.

*The battle may be long, may be hard,*
*but we shall never surrender.*

Something in his blood wanted to leave it at that, though, despite the King. Why go on? Mmm? Always struggling, always alone, hearing voices from the dark. His mother's fingers, irritated, grudging, impatient, somehow called him back from the brink. Finally, ludicrously, it was the rank stench of his father's spit-soaked tobacco which brought him back to himself, sitting suddenly upright, panting as if he had been in a race.

– Sorry –
– None of that! – come along Michael – up you get! it's time to cut your cake!

God's day and Michael's too, thought Arthur, sitting there on the window-seat watching his spindly son blow out the candles. In the man's jacket-pocket was the delicate pressure of a slim, much-thumbed volume of poetry, bought for three-pence in another world before the war. What were those words he had read with bewildered joy on the train that very morning?

*Helpless among the living and the dead,*
*Like a cold water among broken reeds*

And it was a Welshman, by God, who wrote it.
– What's that you're mumbling, Arthur?
Arthur shot an innocent smile towards his wife.
– Nothing, love.
– Really?
– Really!

Violet stared moodily. Off on all his stupid thoughts again! And such a bad liar! Why can't he be like other men strolling up from the club, with their easy grins and banter! As if it wasn't bad enough, after what happened to poor – But there she stopped herself as always, for it was not safe to think such things, especially on Christmas day. Lilly, meanwhile, busy with the washing-up, was making a soothing clatter of plates and dishes which made Vi yawn and let slip of everything for the moment. Michael, picking up cake-crumbs with a wet forefinger, had noticed the moment between his parents, despite the weariness that came after his collapse. But now it was getting dark and the boy felt the comfort that comes with the end of the day. Lilly opened a crack of window to let out some of the fire's heat. From outside, a faint carol. A dog-bark. The squeal of a baby.

– Well, then.
– So soon?
– Train leaves, thirteen-minutes-past.
– Oh, yes. So it does.

And so Violaceae was up from her chair with brisk purpose, winding a woollen scarf three times around her son whilst her husband fumbled with bags laden with divers culinary gifts. Innumerable kisses and hugs on the doorstep. Arthur and Violet took one hand each of their diminutive child and strode down the terraced street, past blunted shapes of Chapel and pithead, towards the station.

– Well, that's that then.

On the train home, Michael caught a speck of soot in his eye, straining out of the window to catch a last glimpse of his ancestral home. His mother applied the corner of her handkerchief with cruel efficiency whilst the boy wailed and squirmed. Opposite, Arthur stared down at his folded hands.

Christmas night. Let her have her way.

Finally the train halted and they stepped off, just a mile or so from Ivy Cottage. A night wind had come up to swirl about the dark Penlan slopes, bringing human and animal sounds, in eddies. Another carol. Another dog. Another wailing infant.

They walked home, rubbing gloves together to make a show of

warmth. Now that night had come there was a smell of hot stoves and roasting chestnuts as they wandered through the village. No words between them. They were just too tired. At last they were back in the house. Violet fussed with the front-room fire as Arthur wiped his lenses clean of Clydach grime. Young Michael pulled off his shoes and stood for a moment by the kitchen window, staring out towards that blackness which was the well. Was she there, still? His father's hand, suddenly, on his shoulder.

– Better now?
– Yes.
– That's good.

That was the end of Michael's thirteenth birthday, Christmas Day, 1942. Arthur was the last to go up to bed. He had prevaricated with vague waves of his hands and his wife had left him to it, with one of her impatient shrugs. And so he stood there, all alone, in the kitchen doorway, contemplating the night. He lit a match carefully on a bit of outside wall. The tiny flame flared long enough for him to suck on his briar luxuriously. Yes, it had been a good day, on the whole, despite Michael's turn. Vi hadn't been so bad, either. He had even heard that old girlish lilt, once or twice, joking with her sisters at the dinner-table.

What would next year bring? A finish to this endless bloody war? And what would happen to little Michael? Arthur remembered his son's magic with the radiogram and took heart. Despite his fainting, the boy was surely growing up, getting past things finally. At that comforting thought, Arthur felt again the warm sensation which was the slim volume of poetry still sitting there in his left-hand pocket. The man took out the book, thumbed through with love and care. Finally, the marked-down page, too dark to read the words, but he remembered them, all the same.

*Rain, midnight rain, nothing but the wild rain*
*On this bleak hut, and solitude, and me*
*Remembering again that I shall die*
*And neither hear the rain nor give it thanks*
*For washing me cleaner than I have been*
*Since I was born into this solitude.*

Violaceae was too far away to hear her husband's recitation, and so Arthur ventured the final lines, louder, out into the night and the beech trees and Penlan Hill – and even to that silent weight of well-water down there, deep in the dark Welsh earth.

# *Meetings*

*The Fourth Station. Our Lord meets his Blessed Mother.*
*"Sweet Jesus, by the Sorrow Thou didst experience*
*Grant me the Grace of a devoted Love . . ."*

The war years continued slowly. Then Michael unexpectedly gained his General School Certificate to the utter delight of both his parents. Secondary School had never been easy, but the boy was good at listening and studying even if he was quiet as the grave in class. The marks were not dramatic, but they were good enough. In a flush of enthusiasm Arthur encouraged his quiet young teenage son to stay on for a Higher National Certificate. Who knows? One day the boy might get a steady, respectable job like his own.

Michael was altering inside, too. One sunny spring day he suddenly decided to wander up into Penlan wood. It was the first time he had been there alone since Annie died. Would the darkness of the trees come and swallow him up? No. Nothing like that. Instead, just a hiss of birch branches and the squawk of a blackbird. Michael said nothing to his parents that night. But as he sipped his tomato soup in the kitchen there was another comforting warmth spreading inside.

Two weeks later Michael returned to the same spot with Timmy, a ginger-headed youth who was the nearest thing he had to a best friend. It was the end of a fine, still day, everything in a drowsy stupor, waiting. They reached dusky woodland above the stream. Both stopped, stood. What was that? The snap of a twig? A wave of fear went through both the boys. Was it the boogie-man who lived in the woods? Or was it one of those filthy tramps?

It was said there were lots of them once, living under the trees, only coming down to village doorsteps for the odd lump of salt or rasher of bacon to cook over their open fires. What made them do it? A few had lost their minds in the Somme, so the teachers said. Others, bare-fist fighting for beer-money high up on Penlan crag. But mostly they were drift-miners who'd got tired of wives and children and started to live in the very caves they'd once tunnelled in the earth. Lonely souls, hardly meriting the fear and prejudice of the village.

A dash of feet away into the tall grass.

– Timmy! Timmy!

Michael turned back, faced the gloom manfully alone. There it was again, where he had first glimpsed it, moments before. Pale as a peeping primrose, and oddly bright next to the muddy farm-track.

What was it?

The gangling youth stepped forward, bent, peered in wonder. Something small and rubbery he saw now. Full to the brim with a pale viscous liquid, like cream on top of the bottle, at school.

– A Frenchie. stupid!

Tim was suddenly back, grinning wickedly. In his hand a hastily-cut hazel-wand which he now manipulated with surprising expertise, like some deep-sea fisherman, plucking the Frenchie aloft, until it dangled high, a yellow candle-flame in the twilight.

– This is nothing! Seen loads down by the canal.

The flame fell to the ground. Timmy was smiling rather oddly, now. Michael felt his friend's cold fingers inside the left leg of his short-trousers, searching inquiringly.

– Feel anything, Mike? Does it ever get big?

Fear took hold before Michael had time to think. And he was all at once racing through the gathering darkness, careless of whipping branches and tangled briars until, twenty minutes later, he could no longer hear Timmy's shrill cries. At last, looking down fern-clad slopes Michael saw with a wash of relief the lights of Ivy Cottage, ruddy and welcoming.

– Where've you been, then, boy?

Michael was blushing furiously, but Arthur didn't notice, knocking his pipe out on the blackened hearth.

A week later Michael returned alone to the woods and the farm-track where the Frenchie lay. Timothy Evans was best-friend no more. And no more yellow primroses today. The boy wandered down through slopes of slender birch-trunks, kicking up piles of leaves. Yes, there it was at last, that pale, weather-worn limestone outcrop which was still familiar from years before. Creeping up, Michael stopped before the cave-entrance, hardly wider than a boy, from which proceeded an icy coldness which seemed to enter right inside. Kneeling low the youth peered into the black, trying to gauge depths and proportions. It was at that moment, stretching his head further, with cobwebs and leaves tickling his neck, that Michael heard her, coming up from miles below.

*Mikey! Mikey!*

The war ended unbelievably, and, taken up by the new national mood, Michael went on at school for his Higher National Certificate, just as his father had hoped. One day, pacing with Arthur through Cardiff's crowded Queen Street, Michael passed a handsome young man impatiently waiting at a newspaper kiosk. Their eyes met, for just a moment. Yet time enough for Geraint Morris to peer curiously into that vivid, lapis lazuli blue . . . Then Arthur tugged his son onward. This was Geraint's first meeting with his future patient, yet he recalled no further details of the incident years later, a fact which is hardly surprising given that the young man was on that very day about to leave Wales for a famous London medical school

Michael's trip to Cardiff was not his first. Indeed, much to his parents' gratification, the young teenager seemed to be beginning to take an interest in all those simple pleasures which characterised the early, escapist postwar days. *Dead Men Walk*, came at last to South Wales in the autumn. A gothic melodrama well suited to the times, the film starred Mary Carlisle and George Zucco, both hugely popular with younger audiences. Michael begged his parents to be allowed to go and see it. Arthur was doubtful. Something inside him remained habitually uneasy. Despite Michael's progress, his son had never been to the cinema. And the boy could still be unpredictable with new experiences. How would he react to watching a horror-picture like that in a strange, crowded auditorium?

– You and your worries! Don't be so selfish! Let the lad go!

Arthur contemplated his wife across the twilit living-room. Her permed hair now rode in tight grey waves across her scalp. Skin lay in heavy folds beneath layers of home-knitted wool. Where was that lithe young creature with her mischievous lapis lazuli eyes? Where was the Violaceae he had loved to utter distraction?

– Maybe, love.

– No maybes! Go tomorrow!

– Right you are, then.

Next day, Arthur buttoned and belted his son's mackintosh and the two tramped out of Ivy Cottage into a veil of rain. Michael had never been so talkative. All the way to the Empire in that hot third-class compartment he was chattering away about the film. Ever so real, they all said! Those vampires make you go hot and cold at the same time! Arthur half-listened, nodding, puffing at his pipe, gazing beyond the glass out at a bleary autumn world.

They arrived at the picture-house on time, but hadn't reckoned on the length of the queue, nor on the somnolence of the ticket-girl who doled out change, counting out each ha'penny on her thick, sweet-stained fingers. Finally, both sweating, they took their seats in the second row, with the music of the film's opening already shrill in their ears. It had been years since Arthur had gone to the pictures. Neighbours muttered in irritation as the man laboriously helped his son to free himself of his soaking coat, then meticulously wiped his pebble-lenses dry with a corner of a sleeve. At last, they were both settled and Michael blinked up at the screen, taking in its blaring enormity for the very first time.

It was just a few minutes later, as Zucco was making his first back-lit appearance, half-comic, half-chilling, that it happened. Michael's eyes dilated oddly in the smoke-coiled darkness. His arms rose up from the arm-rests, gave a short flurry, like a rag-doll shaken by an angry child. Then he slumped unconscious. Sherbet lemons flew everywhere, like a string of pearls broken across a dance-floor.

– Michael? What is it? Michael!

During an eternity which turned out to be no more than two or three minutes, Arthur stumbled madly through the smoke-filled dark, searching for assistance. Finally he came across the silhouetted corpulence of the house-manager. A brief, shrill altercation, finally resolved. A signal to the projection-box. Lights came up blindly everywhere and the film juddered to a halt amid a storm of jeers, boos and slow-hand-claps. Somehow the half-conscious Michael was helped from his seat, assisted to the Exits, aided by the sweet-stained ticket-girl, now reincarnated as an ice-cream attendant. The entire audience gaped after them, arguably more fascinated than they would ever be by Zucco and his confederates. In the musty orange half-light of the foyer, the boy's eyes finally flickered open.

– Better? Mmm? Want a choc-ice, laddy?

Arthur and Michael found themselves back out in the comforting Welsh rain, gripping two soggy ice-creams, Compliments of the Management. They strode towards the railway station with a show of brisk courage, but the carriage back home was a silent as the grave. Finally, trudging up towards Ivy Cottage's garden-gate, Michael uttered his first words in over an hour.

– Don't let's go there again.

– We shan't, boy, don't you worry.

Michael avoided the cinema successfully in times to come, but the fainting-fits did not entirely go away. Much later, when Michael was questioned about his history, he referred to these experiences rather poignantly as *trouble in my heart and brain.*

Now, as the months went by, Michael was growing into an aloof, averted kind of manhood. Anne's secret presence, which had sustained him through puberty, had faded. Music was still a comfort, however. For hours he would stand in front of the radiogram, waving his arms like some demented concert-hall maestro, as orchestras from every part of the world struggled to keep up. Upstairs meanwhile, those shoe-boxes full of meticulously-labelled stones, were slowly gathering dust. Boys always have their fads, Arthur thought, with a pang of disappointment. Why should my son be different? But the young man was different, oh, so different, and that was the worry and sadness of it. Poor Michael, born so portentously on Christmas day, was not, it seems, like any normal boy at all.

One day Violet had an idea. There they were, husband and wife, shelling peas from the garden onto the kitchen oilcloth, when the woman looked up with a sudden brightness in her eye.

– A bike.
– What, love?
– Are you deaf or something? Give the boy a bike!

Arthur still stared. Vi threw down her dish-cloth in anger and triumph.

– Why not? Mmm? You're superintendent now. We can afford it!

A bicycle. Yes . . . Arthur poured empty pea-shells like green water into an enamel pail. Rising from the table, he walked to the door. Through the window, a still grey evening was on its way. A wood-pigeon cooed softly to its mate from the dimness of the trees. Nearer he could see that a slate had fallen from the well-head. He must fix that tomorrow before the others all got loose.

– Arthur? I'm still waiting!
– Might be an idea.
– Might? Might! It'll do him the world of good, you hear! He needs to get out. Always mooning about the house, under our feet. Go on, now. Get it on Saturday!

Arthur turned to his wife, noticing with a jolt new lines of life and excitement in her face.

– Alright. Saturday morning it is.
– Make sure you don't change your mind!

He didn't. In fact he spent more money than he dared even tell his wife. Thus it was that a week later a gleaming new Gentleman's Tourer got delivered to the house. Arthur leant it against a sun-drenched cottage-wall. How its paintwork and chrome fittings shone in the afternoon light! Violet appeared, pushing a dazed sixteen-year-old before her.

– Surprise! Surprise!

Both parents watched in silence as Michael finally arrived at the spot, to touch the handle-bars with slow, hesitant wonder. Those piano-playing fingers advanced slowly, tried out a rack-and-pinion brake.

– Latest model. Last you a lifetime!

Michael nodded, far away. The sun disappeared into a cloud. Icy cold suddenly swirled about the garden path. Violet drew her bottle-green cardigan tight about her shoulders, pursed her lips, growing impatient.

– Your father paid good money for it, my lad! Well? What do you say?

Michael turned around, gazed at his parents. An unreal smile played over his voluptuous lips.

– Can I try it now?

And so he wobbled off, moments later, down the steep lane, negotiating various boulders and pot-holes with varying degrees of competence. Finally, a small dot in the distance. Arthur and Violet looked at each other, grinned, then went deathly pale.

– The main road! Oh, God!

Arthur was filled with the memory of a ten-ton lorry hurtling murderously across swathes of suburban tarmac. His feet wanted to tear wildly down the lane after his son, but instead life seemed to pause in its diurnal course. Leaves left off their waving, birds and insects froze in their flight, waters went still and silent in all their hidden courses . . .

Then Violet gave one of her quick, dismissive shrugs.

– You can worry about anything if you try hard enough.

With that she stalked calmly back to the house. Arthur was alone. He swallowed hard, struggling to capture some of his wife's strength of mind. From out of nowhere, a jangle of bicycle-bell and screech of rack-and-pinion. There was his son, yards away, flushed face beaming in moving dapples.

– It went great!

Finally the boy stopped beside his bemused father, slewing dramatically, almost crashing into a thicket of brambles.

– What d'you think, dad!

Arthur blinked through damp lenses. His son's face, panting, suffused with pleasure – seemed like a stranger's.

– I'm really glad, boy.

They returned to the house, arm in arm. A week later and Michael was cycling off for the day with thermos and sandwich-box bulging from his saddle-bag. Inside Ivy Cottage, Arthur stood in his son's bedroom, now strangely empty and silent, but still smelling hauntingly of a life that was irretrievably part of his. The forty-year-old man sat on his son's narrow bed, stared up at the shape of Penlan hill, beyond the bedroom window. Suddenly he was back there in his own youth, crouched in a Penclydach attic-bedroom, with the memory of Violaceae's hand, scented with spring flowers, raging. Arthur was not sorry that his boyhood and all its difficulties had gone. But it wasn't just books of philosophy which told him that something is always lost back there, never to be re-discovered, like the trail of a shooting-star. And what of Michael? Would these be the kind of days he would treasure, in his turn?

1947 was coming to its end. In Paris, Peace Treaties were finally being signed. In faraway India, the frail figure of the war-hater, Mahatma Gandhi, would one day soon be cut down by assassins . . . In London, Geraint Morris had qualified as a doctor and got married in a whirl. Twelve months earlier, completing his medical-training, the young man had been made exempt from post-war National Service. The matter had hardly concerned him, for when he wasn't studying obsessively, the ambitious young man had been quick-stepping across a polished dance-floor with his latest flame, this time the woman he loved. Filled with the excitement of marriage and career, there was little time now to give thought to armies and medals and the rest. Instead, thinking back to that long-ago day when a young teenager had lied dramatically to a recruiting officer, Geraint found himself sighing with relief.

Thank God. Now I can make something proper of myself!

Christmas time. Flurries of tiny snowflakes, the kind that come with the coldest season, filled that dark mesh of beech-branches around Ivy Cottage with a strange, silent white. All Christmas Eve Michael had been restless and fretful. Today was his eighteenth birthday, but it would be the last he would spent at home in a while. Just a few weeks before, formal notice had arrived from the Ministry of War, informing Michael's parents of their son's Conscription. The enlistment-date was but a few short months away. After that Michael would be away from home for two whole years.

At first the boy had been full of nervous excitement at the news, despite the enormity of the change. To leave home, put family tragedy, worry and isolation behind him! To be independent at last, brave and manly like all those other young soldiers who had fought so valiantly for their nation's victory! Whizzing on his bicycle down the mountain road at over twenty miles an hour, this dream of freedom and happiness brought tears to his eyes and Michael found to his surprise that he was giving great war-whoops to the oaks and sycamores that flew past.

But now, on a grey Christmas dawn, filled with a mass of tiny snowflakes, Michael felt the terror of upheaval, like an icicle forming right there next to his heart. The tic had come back, in its train, shivering beneath his left eye. Michael threw back the bedclothes, padded downstairs, counting those fourteen steps for comfort, as always. Suddenly he stopped. Violet was there, despite the early hour, standing in the hallway, fixed in silent thought. Michael had never seen her like this, as she was to herself. He froze. Finally she noticed, looked up. For a moment the young man glimpsed naked misery on her face. Then it was gone, replaced by that more familiar sullen rage.

– How long have you been watching me!

Hastily remembering the day and recovering herself, her lips made the semblance of a maternal smile.

– Merry Christmas, lad.

– Merry Christmas mam.

Michael stumbled past his mother into the reassuring light of the kitchen. On the yellow oilcloth was a game of solitaire, half-finished. How long had she been up, playing? Violet arrived behind, briskly gathering up the cards.

– Light a fire in the front-room, now there's a good boy.

He did the job quietly and efficiently, glad to be away from his thoughts. Half an hour later, returning the coal-bucket to the garden shed, the young man heard an odd sound behind him, like the scampering feet of a child. He looked back and saw against the lawn's snowy smoothness the stark shape of an old, greying fox.

The fox remained utterly still. Man and animal gazed at each other for what seemed an eternity across the blank silence of the snow. Then, with a proud toss of his brush, the creature turned, loped casually off across what remained of the lawn, leaving a trail of black pin-holes behind. He was gone. Michael breathed at last. Foxes lived everywhere about the mountain, of course, but they so rarely came down to the valley and the life of men. And never once had one come to Ivy Cottage before. Why now at Christmas? Why today on his birthday? Was it a sign? The boy wandered forward, stared down at the neat paw-prints in the snow. Then he saw it. A tiny speck of vivid red. Another. Another . . .

The animal had been in a fight, or had maybe got caught in a trap. Cold, weak, desperate for food, it had come down to the village, and to Michael. If only he could have helped! Now it was too late. An odd splashing interrupted the boy's thoughts. He looked back at the house and saw his father, stretched out of the landing-window, trying to unfreeze an outside pipe with a boiling kettle. The air between them was filled with a strange mixture of ivy-leaves, steam and snowflakes. Father and son paused, nodded at each other through the mist.

– A fox! On our lawn.

– Really? Now there's a thing!

– He was bleeding, dad.

Arthur could think of nothing to say to that. Looking down, now, like an actor trying to remember his lines. His son's eyes were still on him, two clear pools.

– Will he die?

Arthur made an effort, met his son's gaze, shook his head with cheerful confidence. Was that the moan of an injured animal, high up, now, on Penlan hill? Probably just the wailing of wind and trees. Arthur took off his glasses, wiped them clear of steam and melting flakes. Down the village lane somewhere the British Home Service was playing *All Through the Night*. Already there was a smell of nutmeg and pork crackling. Violet appeared on the front doorstep, wiping her hands vigorously on a towel.

– Come on in, now! Don't you want your presents?

They gave him a pile of gramophone records that year, each protected by its own dark-blue cardboard sleeve. All his favourites were included. Schubert, Mozart, Brahms. He took each one out, gazed at the maze of shiny grooves.

– Funny. All that music trapped inside.

That Christmas night, mother and father sat watching their only son as he bent over his new collection, polishing each disc reverently with a chamois. Then, finally, he set one upon the radiogram spindle. Cellos and horns rose up magically and filled the house, banishing all memories of snowy wastes and dying animals. Michael knelt next to the loudspeaker, his long legs oddly contorted on the carpet. Watching his son's arms swaying to the music, Arthur remembered the enlistment-date, just a few short months off. There, in an inside-pocket, were the War Ministry papers still, with his neat signature of consent at the bottom.

– Perhaps there's time to stop them. What d'you think, Vi? Shall I write to the Ministry?

Violet stared up from her darning basket. Not tonight! Not on Christmas day! Arthur pushed his spectacles back up his nose, coughed, tried for a more seasonal brightness.

– Which one is this, then, Michael?

– Schubert's Sixth.

– Ah, yes. Mmm. Of course.

Violet's thin smile, down again at her sewing.

– How about a bit of something lighter, mmm? Now and then? *Don't Fence me in* or *Swinging on a Star*.

Her laughter, quick and uneasy, before the Schubert crescendo took over. Arthur gazed again at his son, so absorbed by the music. It was all so stupid. What would he do in an army? As if in answer, a thirty-year-old memory suddenly welled up in his imagination in the form of a clatter of conscripts' boots over Penclydach cobbles. So many frail forms, like tree-trunks in a plantation. All cut down! But no. It couldn't be like that any more. Not now. Not after two World Wars.

In such ways Arthur sought to reassure himself over the days and weeks that followed. And yet a dull fear stubbornly remained. Bent over a frozen-up well-head on a grey January afternoon, the man suddenly felt a stab. The lad still has trouble tying his shoelaces! How will he survive? But by then it was far too late. The Army Medical Board had written the week before, with its pronouncement.

*Fit for Service. Category One.*

1948 dawned. Michael's enlistment date approached remorselessly and Arthur found himself instinctively suppressing his fears.

– After all, it's not as if you have any choice in the matter, is it?

Shortly before his departure, Michael was given a full army medical, including the statutory PULHEEMS test. Notes made by the supervising MO referred to the boy's bitten-down nails and pale complexion – disclosing a new detail, which even his parents hadn't quite noticed.

*Stammers slightly, upon excitement.*

Despite these and other *minor instabilities,* Michael was pronounced fit and the necessary documents were duly signed and forwarded to Aldershot camp. In less than a month, Michael would join the Royal Army Ordnance Corp for eight weeks' basic training. Sitting in his spacious new GPO Superintendents' Office one fine spring afternoon, Arthur stared across at a pencilled ring he had etched onto the wall-calendar, and felt sick with impending loss.

– Think of something else. Friday dinner. Sausage and mash. I hope Vi browns the onions this time.

Early March. Enlistment was just a week away. Michael's face possessed a shiny pallor of excitement. His eyes seemed permanently dilated. Arthur watched the way his son's knife scraped margarine again and again across his breakfast toast and felt his fists tighten on the table.

– Stop that, now, boy, you're spreading that toast to death!

Michael's knife stopped, but he didn't seem to pick up the fear in his father's voice. Too full of all that the Recruitment Officer had been telling them about Induction Week.

– There's talks and demonstrations and slide shows – !

Inside Michael, a joy spreading like early-morning sun across grass. No more hot schoolrooms! No more boys pointing mocking fingers! Michael's knife started layering thick-cut marmalade onto the toast, on and on and on . . . Across the table Arthur and Violet stared at their son in astonishment.

– Hold on, there, lad.

– Oh – right! – so—rry – !

Was it then that they first recognised the tiny stammer in his voice? But the boy was already rising from the table, wandering out into a sunny back-garden. The slam of the door. Murmur of wood-pigeons. The two parents were alone, contemplating their son's toast, untouched, soaked with all that margarine and marmalade.

– D'you think he might – ?

Violet rose, scooped up the toast, thrust it into the bin.

– He'll be fine, you hear? Fine!

– Mmm. Of course.

Later, in the black heart of a Penlan night, Arthur woke with a lurch from a dreamless sleep. Rising from bed, he wandered unsteadily to the window. That familiar hiss of beech-branches. He glanced down to the other piece of darkness which was the garden-well and remembered a day, many years before, when he had crouched there, next to a gangling seven-year-old.

Was it her? Was it Annie's voice they'd heard?

The evening before Michael's departure the family sat down for a celebratory meal of fish and chips and processed peas. Outside, it was raining, which was somehow comforting, as if all that water could wash away their fears. But then, towards ten, when Michael rose from his chair to go up to bed, Arthur found himself clutching his boy's awkward frame with sudden emotion.

– Goodnight, boy.

– Goodnight, dad.

Arthur felt his son's palms for the briefest of moments on his bare arm. They were ice-cold. He remembered them for years after.

– Write home, now, don't forget!

– I won't.

A few agonisingly short hours later, Arthur and Vi stood on the railway-station platform watched their son's frail form, fast disappearing from view. The cold hand that had touched his father last night now waved with mad excitement as the train accelerated into the distance. Finally there was just silence and grey sky and the lingering smell of coke.

– Oh, well. That's that.

Man and woman turned in unison, trudged back to the house. Glad of Ivy Cottage's dusty twilight, Arthur busied himself with a pot of tea. Violet laid out cards for solitaire. The lines on the table were so straight, today, so mathematical, her husband thought, as he went outside with the kettle. Winding up a pail of fresh well-water, Arthur tried recollecting images of two happy figures racing hazel-twigs down a woodland stream. Still the fear would not quite go away.

A week went by, like an age. No news from Aldershot. When Sunday finally came around Arthur restlessly paced the house for an hour, then stood with decision before his wife.

– Think I'll make a day of it. Take the boy's bike. Brecon Beacons, maybe, if my legs will get me that far. What d'you think?

– Suit yourself! You always do.

And so Arthur hacked himself a few ill-shaped Marmite sandwiches, filled a thermos with dark tea and was soon speeding his way north through windy April sunshine, towards the Heads of the Valleys.

– Beats all that thinking!

The man was discovering, like his son before him, how vigorous pedalling can erase many of the anxieties of the world. A few short hours later he looked up, panting and sweating from all those inclines, and saw to his surprise and pleasure that he was already past Merthyr Vale and nearing those bare mountain scarps beyond. Another forty minutes of dogged toil brought him to the Storey Arms, a whole two thousand feet above sea-level. He was fitter than he thought! Here Arthur halted for lunch, wandering away from the road towards a piece of sheltered heather where sheep cropped lazily and a brook foamed dreamily across trails of sun-bleached rock.

Biting into his make-shift sandwiches, the man felt a surge of joy and freedom. A dizzy scent of grass and bracken-stems and sheep-shit took away all the fretfulness which had imprisoned him for weeks. If only he could lie here on this sunny bank forever! Staring across green-blue vistas, Arthur thought of all the things he might still do before he died. Foreign travel. Books. Concerts. Those poems he had always wanted to write! Suddenly the man felt that there was nothing he could not achieve, if he dreamt hard enough. Here, looking over the dizzy landscape, everything seemed possible, easy even. And at this moment, as they had done so many years ago on a Penclydach street-corner, tears of joy sprang in Arthur's eyes, blurring all that was.

– It's not too late!

On his way back, Arthur took a bend too fast in his weariness, and found himself sprawled in a forest of stinking alder-stems, both arms grazed and his GPO pocket-watch stopped forever at two-minutes-past-four. He somehow clambered back aboard the bike, straightened a bent mud-guard, and proceeded onwards with more circumspection, finally arriving back at Ivy Cottage just as a delicately-horned moon was beginning to peep over Penlan hill.

To his surprise, Violet was not to be found in the house. Arthur wandered back out into the gloom of the garden, finally discovered his wife, there, leaning at the wicket-gate.

– What is it, love?

– Don't know.

Surprised by the softness of her voice, he came close, touched her arm in the darkness. Suddenly they were in a tight embrace, the moon popping dizzily in and out of view. A whisper, hot in his ear.

– So scared – see – don't know why.

– It'll be alright, Vi – you'll see.

But it wasn't. Five weeks later, in the early hours of a May Sunday morning, the couple were woken by a loud hammering on the front door. Arthur stumbled downstairs, pulling on his dressing-gown. Finally, still in a daze of sleep, he threw back the door. A dark form blundered past him, moaning wildly, and filling the house with a gut-wrenching stink.

*Like a wild beast*

It was that phrase of Arthur's, Geraint Morris recalled years later, which got to the heart of it. For it so precisely described what their son had now become.

## *The Helper*

*The Fifth Station. Simon of Cyrene helps our Lord.*
*"Most beloved Jesus*
*By Thy grace I will not refuse to carry the Cross;*
*I accept, I embrace it . . ."*

Geraint Morris got married within a few short months of qualifying as a doctor. It all seemed to happen in such a wild flurry, which troubled his parents back home in Wales. But when they finally met Zina off the London train, she charmed them almost as much as she had her future husband. All their objections melted into nothing.

Growing up in Dominica there was more than a touch of the exotic in her nature, which drew out an unexpected passion in the young man. She was beautiful, he told his medical college pals, but it wasn't simply that. There was fire and wit and mystery! They sniggered over their brown ales and wandered home to leave him on a Holborn street corner, dreaming of his foreign princess.

They were engaged while he was studying for his final exams; but Geraint was happy, even then, to give up one or two of his old ambitions for the sake of true love and married bliss. Gone were those dreams of famous surgeon, admired consultant, inventor of a host of wonder-cures . . . Instead he would settle for general practice – and back home, too, in South Wales.

Yet there were old ghosts still lurking obscurely within the young man that needed their freedom. And so it was just two months before the wedding that Geraint found himself clambering alone onto the train from Paddington to Fishguard with a hiker's heavy kit-bag strapped to his back.

– Time to think. You need to make that pause sometimes in your life, don't you?

The young man arrived in a breezy West Wales that same

afternoon, his pulse calmer than it had been in a while. Free of the city at last, he shifted his pack firmly on his back, went into a quick, determined stride, climbing out of Fishguard town towards the coast-path, thence to trek south towards the grey mystic rocks of St Davids.

Geraint reached the cliff-path by mid-afternoon, remembering it vividly from his childhood days, though his family were never ones to forage more than a half a mile of coastline before returning home for supper and a soft bed. The wind had dropped somewhere back there where the terraced houses had ended. Now the summer sun beat hard on the land, and the earth had become so hot he could feel its charge rising through his boots right up into his calves. The canvas-pack which felt light and easy a short half-hour ago now bore down through his damp shoulders towards the pit of his stomach. Runnels of sweat dribbled down his nose and neck. Yet how the sea dazzled and shimmered! And how huge and vivid everything seemed after the noise and grime of South Kensington!

Geraint must have trekked a couple of hours like this, in a hot, blundering, trance. Finally he came to a twisting descent, bordered by fronds of fern, gorse and bramble, many higher than a man. Below the young doctor now, the darker shapes of wind-stunted oak, ash and hazel, where a stream must have cut deep into the cliff. With a surge of new energy he hurried forward. Sheltered from the strongest rays of the sun, the flies found him, and soon there was a whole angry cloud of them, whirling in front of his reddened, sweat-clogged eyes. Waving arms about like a madman, Geraint found himself breaking into a half-run, back-pack rocking dangerously – until there he was suddenly in a rich darkness heavy with the scent of oak and alder and wild garlic.

Stillness. A strange, dream-like gap. Then a moving brightness in front of his exhausted vision. Of course. It was a stream! And at that moment, quite magically, the young man was down on his hands and knees beside it, dipping his fingers into that shocking iciness with primitive urgency. Careless of germs and parasites and the rest he bathed his burning face, drank deep.

A few hours later Geraint found a camping place on a sheltered fold of cropped pasture, not far from the formidable blue dolerite of

Strumble Head. Darkness was already falling over a calm expanse of Irish sea, casting apocalyptic patterns of pink and mauve. In his sudden haste to get out of the city he hadn't checked his borrowed tent. There were a few panicky moments, therefore, staking out the canvas in correct order. Had his friend forgotten anything? Lost a vital peg? No, he hadn't, thank God. Finally it was set, roof taut, entrance-flaps rippling comfortingly in the first of the evening breezes. Feeling the cold of the night already underneath his shirt, Geraint crawled quickly inside, dragging his kit in after him.

Should he have left his darling Zina behind. Should he? No, you were right to come here alone, Geraint.

Supper over, he lay back exhaustedly on top of his sleeping-bag, absorbed at last the mesmerising tidal wash of the sea some fifty feet below, felt his eyes close heavily. The Irish Sea roared on, washing over all that ever was. Geraint felt himself drowning, inch by inch. Finally he was asleep.

An age later, pulling back the tent flaps, the young man gazed blearily out at the dawning world and his heart leapt. Without yesterday's heat and all that dizzy, mind-numbing exhaustion, everything was transformed, many times more wondrous. Stretching aching limbs, Geraint stared south past veils of rain-cloud, towards those low, mysteriously-shaped hills around St David's head. After London's cramped maze of streets, the sense of space was breath-taking. He waited for it to dissolve, like some dream – but, no, it stayed, even got clearer as the morning light progressed, so that soon he could distinguish a pattern of cliff and field and pasture, surmounted here and there by the craggy remains of a Cromlech or Iron Age hill-fort. A mewing cry, unexpectedly close. He looked up to see a gull sailing calmly past, inches away, hugging the cliff-edge updraughts. Man and beast exchanged glances, like fellow travellers in the tube. The bird's eyes seemed wise, patiently appraising. Then, suddenly he was on his way with a flick of tail-feathers, moments later a pale dot over the restless, white-flecked sea.

Geraint lit his Primus stove and breakfasted on bread, cheese and deliciously sweet tea. An hour later, he was journeying south once more, the straps of his pack beginning to chaff at yesterday's sore places. Despite the cloud-cover, yesterday's oppressive August heat was coming back, stronger by the moment, so that after a mile or so, he was wiping huge dribbles of sweat from his forehead with the edge of his sleeve.

Then it happened. Geraint hit the ground so suddenly, he had no idea then or years after what did it. Somehow he left his pack behind and was slithering and somersaulting downwards helplessly, gorse branches whipping past in a blur. The young man made ineffectual grabs at various rocks and bushes and tufts of grass along the way, but nothing seemed to stop him. Terror leapt up at his throat. How far was he from the edge? The angry grey of the sea seemed to rise ever nearer . . .

In a dream Geraint finally groped at a piece of decaying bramble-root – and somehow, miraculously, held on. The world slowed, stopped its wild turning. His panic-stricken panting finally returned to something close to normal. Raising himself arduously to a sitting-position, he saw with a lurch of horror that he was just a few short feet from the edge. A dull throbbing from somewhere low down told him that his ankle was badly sprained at least, or broken. Tears sprang to the young doctor's eyes from somewhere.

Dear God – !

He tried to gather his thoughts logically. Above him, just a smear of green and grey which was the hillside. Faintly, a dark pencil-line which was the path he had been walking moments ago. Now all that seemed an age away. The pain of the fall and the injured leg began to sear through him, taking his breath away. He calculated that the coastal track lay a good fifty feet above. It was clearly best to sit tight and wait rather than risk making matters worse by moving. Surely another hiker or farmer or local fisherman would come along in time. None did, however. Geraint lay there for several long hours, in dull agony. Finally, with the sun descending rapidly over the sea he began to have second thoughts. Was there any point in staying here, on the edge of oblivion? The doctor steeled himself for heroic action, began to make beetle-like, pain-racked movements, inch by inch from that nightmarish precipice – up towards the comforting brown blob which was the shape of his faraway canvas-pack lying a few feet from the path.

After half-an-hour or so he met a cigarette packet. The young doctor made a habit of never smoking in the day. Smiling wryly to himself therefore, Geraint managed to perch one broken cigarette between his lips, lighting it with a box of matches which had miraculously survived the tumble. The nicotine revived his spirits. He resumed his insect-like ascent with renewed efficiency. But now the pain in his left foot possessed an energy of its own. And then, without warning, the rain came, animated by rumbles of thunder, ominously big-dropped. At first Geraint was relieved and refreshed after the heat of the day and his pain-filled exertions. But then, as the slope became quickly transformed into a slimy morass, his mood began to change. Fear took hold and the young man began to scramble blindly forward, digging his nails deep into the slithery mud, searching for a grip. Now, at a stroke it seemed, it was dark. As if the torrential rain wasn't enough, gusts were now buffeting at him, threatening to tear his body right off the glassy slope. Geraint wanted to scream out, but didn't have the strength. Instead, he seemed to watch himself in mute terror, as he clutched blindly at the yawning precipice. Any moment, he might start once more that fateful slide. He had to go on. His broken fingers dug deeper into the liquefying earth, past all normal pain. He dragged up one limb, a few inches, then another. Somehow, impossibly, he was still going forward.

Zina. Oh, God, Zina!

At some nebulous point the young doctor must have lost everyday consciousness, for later he had no memory of finally meeting his canvas pack. But reach it, he did. And then, perhaps half-an-hour later in the black of night, he must have got his sodden, pain-twisted body somehow back onto the safety of the path, although he recollected nothing of that either. Once on the path he must have fallen immediately into a pit of sleep.

A shrapnel-like fragment of blue dolerite digging into his cheek finally brought Geraint back into the waking world, hours later. He lifted his head drunkenly, glimpsed a blaze of rain-sodden gorse slopes, heard a din of wheeling sea-birds – and found himself weeping uncontrollably. An hour later he found the strength and ingenuity to unpack his kit and boil up a cup of black tea on his

Primus. The taste of that simple brew seemed like the very savour of life.

The rain and wind were finally all gone. It was time for Geraint to make a sober assessment of his situation. A professional examination of his ankle revealed that is was swollen badly and ominously dark with bruising. But that attenuated throb of pain suggested it was a sprain, not a broken bone. Strapping the injury carefully with strips of torn-up shirt, Geraint managed to jam his foot back into his boot. Somehow he was just able to stand. So far, so good. But what about the distance and the weight of the pack?

Late morning by the angle of the sun. The air was bright and fresh with white clumps of cloud sailing by like kindergarten cut-outs. Geraint meticulously prepared for the road, lightening his kit by disposing of various inessential items. Would it be easier and simpler to go back to Fishguard? It was hard to tell distances, but something deep down in the young man wanted to go on with his journey, whatever the cost.

At first, things progressed well enough, as Geraint advanced slowly, patiently picking out each foothold in the uneven surface of the coastal path. Almost noon. The day was sunless, but still very warm. The heat began to press down on his scalp like a punishing hand. How much longer before he reached civilisation? Geraint blinked into space, through rivers of sweat, praying for some sign, even the humblest farmhouse. By now the young man was close to the wilds of Pwll Deri, trekking across great masses of volcanic rock, four hundred feet or more above the lead-grey roar of the sea. Where was that hostel his friends had told him about? Nowhere to be seen.

Near Porth Maenmelyn Geraint had another bad moment, swaying uncontrollably where the coastal path became little more than a narrow ledge at the summit of a perilous cliff-face. Sick with relief and exhaustion, he finally cleared the worst of the terrain, lay down on a hammock-like shape of couch-grass. Finally the slow murmur of the sea calmed him.

Oh, Zina. What was I doing? Why on earth did I come here?

An hour later Geraint reached a small whitewashed cottage in the middle of nowhere. He stared in a dream at its neat garden, filled with a dazzle of rose-blossom. Somewhere back there the young man had lost his water-bottle. He was parched with thirst. He knocked loudly on the door. The woman who answered looked small and frightened in the dimness of the porch. Geraint nodded politely, slumped unconscious to the ground. Later the doctors told him that the woman had somehow dragged him inside, still strapped to the heavy pack. Later he had a vague memory of a room filled with the yellow light of electricity, and the sound of someone murmuring urgently into a heavy bakelite phone. She must have called the police before the ambulance, because his first firm recollection was of a constable's stiff, buttoned-down uniform, towering over him. He was taken by car to the nearest hospital, which seemed to be an enormous distance away. There the young man was placed in a quiet side-ward with a view east towards the blue summits of the Brecon Beacons. Three days later Geraint was discharged and driven by ambulance to Fishguard station where a group of surprised-looking fishermen watched as the young doctor was helped aboard the London train, canvas pack and crutches trailing inside the carriage.

Zina's ashen face at Paddington station told him that she knew the worst of his adventures. They crossed the city in silence, finally sat opposite each other at a plain kitchen table.

– Funny. I don't think I was ever as near death. Maybe it'll do me some good. What d'you think?

Zina laughed dryly, gathering up the plates and dishes. But that night Geraint could not get to sleep for excitement. Yes. It was true. He had been changed! Those restless ghosts of his seemed to have been left there with the cliffs and gulls and grey roar of the ocean. And he had confronted a little something of mortality and human suffering, not on the pages of a dry medical text-book, but in his own flesh and blood. What did it matter if he remained a family doctor all his life? If he understood people, if he recognised their experience, their suffering, if he was able to help – was this any the less important than a new cure for diphtheria or polio or the Asian flue?

– I'll remember that day on the cliff. Yes. I'll keep it always with me.

A few months later Geraint and Zina were married and travelling down together to the young doctor's new general practice in South Wales. Zina shocked Geraint by her energetic enthusiasm. If Wales meant for him the familiarity of roots and childhood – for her it was something excitingly different. But there were other unexpressed reasons, too. For Zina shared with Violaceae thirty years before her that yearning for children which could overwhelm the sense. And although she would, of course, have loved fame and fortune and a comfortable life amongst the Kensington elite, she loved this beautiful young man, wanted to share his life wherever he went, whatever he became.

And so one fine spring morning the young doctor and his wife found themselves boarding the Cardiff train at Paddington, surrounded by a jumble of luggage and piles of books tied with string.

Geraint had a dapper urban air about him that day, dressed in the latest Jermyn Street fashion, and sporting the merest artful hint of a moustache. They giggled all the way down to Wales. Geraint had the art of mimicry and gave his new wife a vivid account of the kind of village Welshmen she would be likely to meet, there, at the foot of the mining valleys where the young man had secured his first position.

There followed a nightmarish month, however, cooped up at the parental home in Barry town, with Geraint rushing off to travel twenty miles to his practice each day at the crack of dawn. Finally however, the young man found the perfect home, a mere few yards from the surgery. It was a modest terraced house admittedly, but right next to the river, so that in every room you could hear the bubbling of the weir. They moved in just three weeks later, thanks to a generous cash advance by his father to secure the deal. Zina astonished her husband by transforming the place in small yet imaginative ways so that by the summer you'd have thought they had lived in it all their lives.

Geraint, meanwhile, sought out patients for all he was worth, praying that a combination of pleasant looks, cheerfulness and youthful energy would give him something of an entrance in what was, he knew, an entrenched community. Thankfully the old doctor who preceded him had a love of household brandy which meant that bottles were routinely hidden away at the mere sound of his rusty old side-car motor-bike, approaching up the road. Geraint Morris quickly acquired the reputation of a new broom. A bit flighty, maybe, foppish in his bright London cravats – but possessing a knowledge, enthusiasm and commitment the local community badly needed.

And what was so wrong with strangers from England? They gave you something to gossip about!

When the baby came along soon after, Geraint and Zina were finally and fully accepted. Neighbours came in furtively (for this was still a time of rationing) carrying pats of local Welsh butter wrapped in grease-proof paper. The old lady down the road knitted their 'little Precious' a tiny elfin cap. Even gruff old Mr Edwards from the Post Office who had pointedly ignored them ever since Geraint had made the mistake of playing Glen Miller loudly on a Sunday Morning – tapped on their door one day, handing the astonished Zina a bag of home-grown cooking apples from his garden.

– No. Don't go thanking me. Don't now!

And with that he was scurrying off down the road.

Life became busy for them both, but Geraint and Zina somehow found time (with Geraint's mam lovingly tending the baby) to go for weekend walks in their new-found country home. Growing up in the gentle vales around Barry, Geraint wasn't used to the dim woods of oak, ash and alder which hugged the steep valley slopes in those days before coniferous plantations took over everything. But for Zina this was entirely foreign country, so the young man took it upon himself to be the knowledgeable and enthusiastic guide. They found they shared a love of wild flowers and birds. One day Geraint went down to Cardiff and spent his last few shillings on a Kodak camera and roll of film. A month later, on his way to the chemists to develop yet another expensive roll the young doctor remembered a friend of his at school, passionate about darkrooms, who took him inside his little home-made kingdom, full of strange equipment and even stranger chemical smells.

Perhaps it was that all-but forgotten dream of triumphant

medical investigation, somehow mutated, which lit the flame now. Zina watched in a daze as, over the next week, her husband rushed up and down stairs, carrying a whole pawnbroker's shop of obscure equipment and supplies – bound for the tiny box-room where they had left all their empty luggage-boxes on that first day. Blocking off a small dormer-window, Geraint transformed the space into a faery kingdom, where, just a few short weeks later, he produced his first mysterious images: a cluster of wood anemones, swirling magically into view under a chemical sea. Zina pinned them up with clothes-pegs. A smile flickered on her young, beautiful face. She had caught something of the passion too.

Geraint was framing his first twelve-by-ten print under glass for the living-room, one bright May morning in 1948 when the telephone jangled in the hall.

The frail, confused voice on the other end was a stranger's, for Arthur had yet to register his family with the new general practitioner – and Geraint still knew only one or two of those more secluded folk who lived across the river, at the foot of Penlan hill. But the young man did not pause for an instant. The man's tone told him everything. Forgetting about flowers and photographs and frames he took up his bag and made hurriedly for the front door.

– What is it, love?

Geraint turned for a moment in the garden to smile uncertainly back towards his young wife, tending a row of pansies near the doorstep.

– His son. Just eighteen. Came home from the army last night in a state.

Zina looked up at her husband, shading her eyes against the early summer sun.

– Just think, Zina. He didn't recognise him. Your own flesh and blood. *Like a wild beast.* Those were his words.

And with that the doctor was gone.

# *Comforted*

> *The Sixth Station. Veronica wipes the Face of Jesus.*
> *"Thy face was Beautiful before,*
> *But in this Journey it has lost all its Beauty,*
> *And Wounds and Blood have disfigured it . . ."*

Six weeks before, in late March 1948, Michael had arrived with a lorry-load of other fresh conscripts to join A-Company of the ROAC Training Battalion, at Aldershot Barracks. It was here that basic training was to begin in earnest. Things began to go wrong, almost at once.

The young men arrived, still in their civvies, each gripping his small suitcase of underwear and personal effects. Tumbling out of the canvas-covered trucks in confusion, they only had a few moments to take in a bleak landscape of camouflage-green barracks and Naafi huts, hundreds of them it seemed, each surrounded by its neat border of closely-clipped grass. Michael had been shouted at once or twice by teachers in the past. But now, as they jumped from the lorry and stumbled towards their billet, the air seemed to be filled with insane, shrieking voices. And what they were saying did not seem to be very nice.

– Move your arse, you great lump of steaming-ugly shite!

In a dream, the eighteen-year-old was handed his regulation kit and army-number (22027623), shoved into a dazzling, white-painted wash-room for the standard hair-cut, strip and cold shower. Half-an-hour later, virtually unrecognisable in crew-cut and khaki tunic, Michael cowered shudderingly on a low, iron bedstead, with those shrill NCO abuses still echoing all around. Perfunctory partitions, no more than a foot or so of grey steel locker between each bed, offered a semblance of privacy. Personal life was annihilated at a stroke. Individual identity and human dignity were next in line.

For some stronger young men, trapped previously by poverty or family or social expectation, this rough, pitiless world may have brought a sense of freedom and exhilaration. But for one such as Michael, it was an immediate and utter catastrophe. Those naive hopes he had cherished, whizzing down the mountain road on his bicycle, were lost within moments. And by the time the barracks-lights went out that night with a loud mechanical clang and he shut his eyes in utter exhaustion, listening to a heart which beat like some wild thing – it was as if all normal life had been driven off, beyond some faraway horizon. Instead, fear lay like a fever, pressing up at his throat.

With some fortitude he warded off the worst of forebodings and even found a little sleep at last. But its healing ministry was short-lived, for a few short hours later, even before light had broken, the boy was hurled back into the horror of the present by a renewal of that barrage of terrifying orders, insults and threats which would become, over the next days, the very air he breathed.

Somehow he got dressed, survived a nauseating breakfast, and began that round of mindless chores, inspections, drills and physical exercises which stood for military basic-training in late-forties, post-war England. As if in some weightless, disembodied state, Michael seemed now to look down and observe a wan, bewildered young man agitatedly polishing an infinity of tunic buckles and clasps and buttons until his fingers ached and his nails were worn to the quick. Nearby, a succession of dementedly angry crew-cut faces, watching for the smallest mistake.

– What are you, laddy?

– Don't know, sir –

– Don't know! Don't know! You are a great lump of steaming-ugly shite that's what you are. Let me hear it, now. What are you – ?

– A great lump of steaming-ugly shite, sir.

The brief redemption of darkness came a second time. On this occasion, however, even the cover of night was no protection. For other, younger voices now came up close, to taunt and insinuate through the thick black. Fresh recruits, just like himself, searching for compensation in their confusion, and, as if performing in some ancient rite, seizing upon the weakest and most vulnerable, as beast of sacrifice. The words slithered up like adders. Michael's left eye began to shiver as never before

– Ever seen such flapping great ears. Hah! Like a sodding elephant!

– And those lips. Just like a girlie! Are you a girlie, mmm, private?

Michael woke up an hour before dawn. The barracks was quiet, almost tranquil. For the briefest of moments he knew a peace that smelt of beech leaves and ivy. Then he felt an oddly disturbing warmth, down there, beneath his legs. Terror rose up in him. In an agony of anxiety he managed to remove the urine-soaked sheet from the mattress and hide it behind a nearby cupboard, without anyone waking up. Later, the air inside the billet seemed to reek of sulphur, yet miraculously no-one noticed in the rush to get dressed and washed. Michael survived therefore, for a few more brief hours, on this his second day of military service, sweating and trembling as he shone his boots again and again and again, with that NCO's voice inches above him shrieking endlessly.

– I want to see that ugly shite of a face in it, laddy! What do I want to see?

– That ugly shite of a face, sir.

At some point in the afternoon, they took a group-photograph of the new squaddies, on the parade-ground, for Company records. Michael's face, in the third row, was oddly tilted as if he were trying to sort out some metaphysical puzzle. Shoulders, hunched, tense. Arms uncannily straight at his side. Mouth, slightly open, as if he were about to speak. But what? And to whom?

Where was Annie now? Where was Ivy Cottage and the well and the swing-seat and the beech trees and Penlan mountain and his mother and father drinking tea at the oilcloth-covered kitchen table? Faded images in some family album, parading dreamily in front of him, before they dissolved to nothing. Yet no tears came to Michael that day or any other that week, for there was no time or place for them in a hell such as this.

– What are you laddy?

– A great pile of steaming-ugly shite, sir.

At last, as was natural and inevitable, Michael broke. On Friday April 2nd (as military-records later showed) Private 22027623 was brought at twelve-hundred hours before the Commanding Officer on a charge under section-40 of the Army Act. Private 22027623 had been called out of line during parade earlier that morning and had been asked by his Corporal why it was he could not drill like the rest. Private 22027623 had replied that *he could not do things when he was being shouted at.*

As he questioned Michael, CO Norton-Inge could not help noticing the young man's strained features and unusual paleness of complexion. A small part of him, still separable from profession and duty, took pity. And so, after the lad was gone from the room, he bit the end of his pencil, stared down at the desk-blotter, decided not to proceed with the charge.

– Take him back down, Johnson. But I want a full medical report.

MO Tisdall was a thin, softly-spoken man, too long in the job to really care. Nevertheless he liked clarity and completeness and so he did a reasonably thorough job on the conscript later that day, noting in his neatly-printed log that Private 22027623 was in a state of *mild mental depression* and that furthermore there was a *lack of mental concentration.* Unsettled somewhat by that intermittent flickering of Michael's left eye, he recommended by way of conclusion that Private 22027623 be examined by an army psychiatrist *at the earliest moment.*

The young man was returned to barracks. That night, in the darkness of a crowded billet, Michael lay on his mattress in a state of such turmoil and confusion that his body began to piss and shit uncontrollably in order to be rid of all that ever was. It is said that personal hygiene is the over-riding obsession of all NCOs. The slightest aberration in this area can result in the agony and humiliation of a public scrubbing, head low in the bowl of the barrack-room latrine. As the stench of Michael woeful evacuations rose, therefore, into the warm Nissen-hut air on that night in early April, 1948, his fate was sealed – and the course of the next five weeks decided.

Private 22027623 was next day brought up again before the CO, and, according to army records, ordered under escort to Cambridge

Military Hospital for immediate admission, pending expert psychological examination. During his two-day stay in hospital, Michael was seen several times by staff psychiatrist Albert Kibblewhite who noted in his log that the patient *gave the impression of being completely lost and totally inadequate for the unsheltered life in the army*. A young, eager professional, Kibblewhite had read bits of Freud, Jung and Adler with enthusiasm during his training some years before, and so he put a number of questions to Michael on his personal history and was struck especially by a story concerning *a visit to a certain local picture-house, which had been followed by a probable case of petit mal*. However the doctor concluded that Private 22027623 had not shown at that time, or now, any *directly psychotic symptomology* and so he concluded that the conscript was clearly suffering from some form of *mild psycho-neurosis*.

Michael was returned to barracks, escorted by Regimental Police, on the morning of April 6th. He was placed in the guardhouse under protective custody although the records made clear subsequently that he was *not under any charge*. Instead, as Norton-Inge noted in his statement, confinement was instigated *purely for reasons of supervision and avoidance of ridicule*. It appears that Michael's comrades in the billet had announced to those that mattered that they could not tolerate another night of pissing and shitting right next to their beds.

According to the CO's account, the NCO in charge of the guardhouse was fully briefed on the young man's immediate history, and *made explicitly aware that Private 22027623 was not on any formal charge*, merely to be kept in a place of confinement for practical reasons. The NCO was further advised that Private 22027623 was to be given light duties during the day, as well as regular exercise-periods in an adjoining yard. Twenty-four hours after admission to the guardhouse, according to the Company Sergeant Major's testimony, the young conscript *lost his balance* on the verandah outside the building and grazed both his hands. This was the only reference made in army records to any physical injury to Michael during the time of his imprisonment.

Ten days later, it appeared that Private 22027623 was stable enough to be released from custody and allowed to return to his former barracks' accommodation. He was still required to report each day to the guardhouse NCO for a continuation of those *light fatigues* performed, it seems, at a suitable distance from his comrades. His kit was formally checked and itemised at the time of his guardhouse release; and instructions were conveyed that Private 22027623 was to be visited daily by the MO who would assess the ongoing situation until such time as a full and final psychiatric report was received from Cambridge Military Hospital.

Towards the end of its later report, the army made certain statements concerning Private 22027623's general treatment during his time at Aldershot. Notable amongst these were the following:

– *Private 22027623 was not physically attacked at any time by either officers or men.*

– *Private 22027623 was not verbally abused or psychologically ill-treated at any time by either officers or men.*

– *Private 22027623 was never kept as a prisoner, simply confined to guardroom quarters for his own protection.*

– *Private 22027623 was never under any sort of charge.*

– *Private 22027623 was at liberty to take up all the usual rights and privileges offered to soldiers held in confinement in such a situations, including the opportunity to write letters to his family. He chose not to do so.*

– *No personal effects were ever removed from Private 22027623's possession without his permission during his time of confinement.*

– *Private 2207623 continued at all times to be in receipt of his regular army pay.*

During the latter part of April, arrangements were made by the CO for the convening of a special Invaliding Board, at which psychiatric reports would be received and assessments made with a view to the subsequent discharge of Private 22027623 from the army on medical grounds. On April 13th, Norton Inge received Albert Kibblewhite's report from Cambridge Hospital. It was recommended by Kibblewhite that Private 22027623 be discharged as permanently unfit for any form of military service on the following grounds.

*Anxiety State. Chronic. Mild. Unspecified.*

A week later the Board met. The hospital report was formally taken as evidence and the psychiatrist's recommendation, duly adopted.

It was a mild, breezy day, somewhere far away outside the boardroom. Michael stood there, neatly attired for the first time in a while, head slightly tilted as it had been during that Company photograph a fortnight or more before. Today, however, a bead of pale dribble seemed to be issuing from one side of his slightly open mouth as he listened to the voices that came to him out of the ether. Only once, towards the end, was he put a direct question.

– Have you suffered any injury, accident or mis-treatment during your time in the army, Private 22027623?

A nudge, close to him. Then a whisper.

– Just shake your head, laddy, mmm?

And so Michael shook his head and there was a general shuffling of papers and scraping of chairs which told him that the decision had been reached and it was all over and he would soon be back in that dark corner of cold wet stone which was his new home.

– Come on, now, Private, time to go, mmm?

By then it was almost as if he welcomed his guardhouse prison. Better to be there, after all, where none of these people could smell him.

*What are you?*

*A great lump of steaming-ugly shite.*

A week later, according to the last page of the army report, Private 22027623 was taken to Aldershot railway station by two senior Regimental Officers at which time he was put on an express-train to London. Here, his contact with the army was at an end. In the early hours of Sunday 15th May, Michael finally reached Ivy Cottage and his parents. What had occurred during those fourteen or so hours between his departure from Aldershot and his final arrival in Wales was something upon which the army later said they could not comment, except to suggest that it was possible that the boy lost his bearings somewhere along the way.

The records concluded with the following short paragraph.

*All sworn evidence used in the compiling of this report remains the property of the War Ministry and, according to law, cannot be disclosed to members of the public without the express permission of the Minister.*

At around 7pm on the evening of May 14th, Edith Dockerill, an office supervisor in her late forties, was walking slowly eastward along Praed Street, just a few hundred yards from Paddington station. Light was starting to fade. It had been quite a warm, balmy afternoon with more than a touch of summer in the air. Mrs Dockerill was rather pleased with herself as well as with the weather around her. Work was going well, despite the eccentricities of Smyles, the senior partner, who managed to confound every management procedure. In fact Edith thought she had handled the situation quite well that very afternoon over the Berrywell case, exploiting a mixture of firmness and deference, always the best thing with the old man.

Reaching the corner of Praed Street and Edgware Road, Mrs Dockerill's stride became light, eager, thinking now of her daughter and the prospect of an excellent dinner of lamb chops and jacket-potatoes the dear child would prepare that night in their small terraced house in Kilburn, so quiet, now, since poor Albert had died. It was at that moment, turning to walk briskly northward, that a tall, gaunt figure shambled past the woman, muttering oddly. In the normal course of things, Edith would have taken little or no notice of the man. London seemed full of strange and unsettling sights, in the years that followed the war, not least in the Paddington and Bayswater area where, not far from where she walked, whole lines of Ladies of the Night were wont to ply their trade, up and down the pavements, as twilight imperceptibly descended.

Perhaps it was her good mood, perhaps it was the unexpectedly delicate face of that shambling young man, mumbling down at the paving stones, perhaps it was the sight, glimpsed momentarily in a May twilight, of that pattern of angry abrasions across the fellow's emaciated hands – at all events, Edith Dockerill did a most unusual thing for her, which was to stop, turn and hail a complete stranger in the street.

– Excuse me – wait a moment!

The tall, swaying young man halted automatically, but did not turn around. Edith hesitated, and went against character and upbringing a second time by making a further overture, this time stepping forward hurriedly along the pavement.

– Lost are you, lovey?

A face, finally turning towards her. Managing a busy solicitor's office in the centre of the city, Mrs Dockerill was accustomed to many of the less comfortable aspects of human life. Yet what she saw on this wild, starved-looking face took the kindly lady aback.

– You alright, are you?

The comatosed creature, who had hours before been referred to solely as Private 22027623, could not at that particular moment recognise the forms of normal human communication. Amidst the din of crazed orders which still criss-crossed his head, Mrs Dockerill's gentle interrogations seemed like the cry of a songbird during a storm – noticed maybe, but hardly taken in. Michael had halted his shambling journey along the pavement simply because Edith's shrill cry behind him had momentarily been mistaken for the scream of yet another demented NCO; and the conscript had learned over the last weeks of captivity to respond immediately to such utterances or risk yet more pain and torment.

Edith, meantime, was waiting politely for an answer to her questions. No reply proceeded from the stranger's mouth. Instead, an odd chattering of teeth, now, accompanied by the appearance of tiny trails of saliva, there, just below his full, womanish lips.

In normal circumstances Edith Dockerill would have now retreated, comforted by the thought of a little extra, maybe, next Sunday in the Church collection. But the office supervisor seemed possessed by a sensation she could neither recognise nor understand. Far from turning from the nauseous sight, she approached nearer, put out a hand, gripped one of those thin, trembling shoulder-blades.

– Now, then, dearie? Can I do anything?

Something in the puzzling softness of these few words finally penetrated Michael's state. As Edith stared, a single tear rose up into the stranger's left eye, rolled down a sunken cheek. The woman hesitated no further. Gripping Michael's arm tightly, she led him hurriedly southwards down the Edgware Road towards a quiet teahouse she knew, just off Marble Arch. Handing a bright florin by way of reassurance to the establishment's burly proprietor, Edith Dockerill guided her charge to a seat at the rear of the premises, away from noise and intrusions. Two cups of tea arrived beside them. Edith looked questioningly, popped three sugars into the young man's brew, to be sure. Fishing in her handbag, Mrs Dockerill found a crumpled packet of Craven A, offered one to Michael. No response. Edith lit one for herself, puffed on it cheerfully. For a brief moment the image of her pretty teenage daughter came back into her mind, along with a plate of chops and vegetables, waiting on a place-mat. Edith shoved these idle fancies aside and proceeded.

– Well, lovey? Want to tell me a bit about it?

Michael's lips made a strange hybrid sound, somewhere between a word and a moan. Edith nodded sagely, by way of encouragement, then leaned forward an inch or two to better distinguish any nascent syllables.

– An –

– Eh? What's that?

– An –

– Mmm? Say it again?

– An – nie –

Edith Dockerill made a show of understanding, nodding vigorously, yet little comprehending the meaning of these two, mantra-like syllables. Yet a little of their significance had conveyed itself in the tone. There was a thoughtful silence, during which both gazed, unfocused, through a haze of cigarette smoke. Michael's face suddenly grew taut, looking past the woman, fear gathering, making bubbles of new spittle at his lower-lip. Edith Dockerill turned to the tea-house window and noticed a group of uniformed men walking casually past towards Hyde Park. Turning back to the young man, and noticing for the first time what looked like a month-old military crew-cut, Edith began to have some inkling of what might be amiss in this poor chap's life.

– Soldier, were you, love?

All of a sudden, Michael's hands were flying this way and that in a whirlwind of terror.

– There, there, now! No need to get in a flap! Simmer down, mmm? You're quite safe, here with me!

Michael's eyes seemed to register Edith Dockerill's compassion for the first time, dilated, incredulous. Within, the young man's injured psyche was making huge leaps in that dark nebula which had become his home. Could this strange human form, intruding suddenly into the nightmare of his existence – could it conceivably be a friend?

His hand fluttered limply back down to the table. Teacups ceased to tremble. Edith waited, patient, knowing it was time to be silent. In the course of the next few minutes, Michael's body, previously so charged with tension, seemed to relax for the very first time. Edith nodded, as if responding to a silent confession.

– You've been through a lot, haven't you?

Again she waited patiently. Again, after a minute or two, there was an important change. This time it was in the form of the tiniest of nods. Edith Dockerill smiled gently.

– Maybe I can help? What can I do, mmm?

– Iv –

– What was that?

– Ivy –

– Ivy! – yes – right – is that a name?

– Ivy – cott –

– Sorry, love – you see, I can't quite get what –

– Ivy cott – age –

The effort had taken all strength out of the boy. Edith Dockerill contemplated her companion's exhausted form, beginning to put together the fragments.

– A house – right? Must be somewhere in the country. Is it where your parents live, maybe, mmm?

A high wail indicated Michael's eager assent. The pieces were falling together quickly now. Edith stubbed her cigarette decisively on the ash-tray.

– I met you next to Paddington didn't I? So you were probably on your way home, somewhere in the west. Spot of leave, maybe? Dorset? Bristol? Or Wales, how about Wales?

Half an hour later, the two new friends reached Paddington station, wreathed in smoke and darkness. Digging into her weekly wages without a second thought, Edith Dockerill found the fare for a single ticket to Cardiff. Walking away from the booking-hall, they sat at a bench, close to platform-one. Above them now, a sea of yellow, electric bulbs, swaying in shifting currents of steam. The din of a departing express-train banished normal conversation. Edith thought back to her brief telephone conversation some minutes before when she had informed her bewildered young daughter of the recent encounter and her plans for the rest of the evening. Strangely, she had neither opposed, nor complained. Edith imagined her now, scraping dried-up meat and potatoes disconsolately into the kitchen bin. Would she understand, deep down, what was happening? Would she?

The express had gone. The station became strangely quiet. Edith offered another of her Craven A's to the young man, just in case. But the boy refused with a blank look, as before. The lady lit her own, stared up at the patterns of yellow bulbs, as if they were stars in a Zodiac.

– Funny thing, life, isn't it?

Michael said nothing. But he seemed to be listening. Edith took another deep, thoughtful puff on her fag.

– Albert was a Navy man, see. Went in at the beginning. But never saw much action, just a couple of U-Boat torpedoes, missing them by a mile. Still, we were both thankful as anything when it was all over, I can tell you. No doubt about it, war, even when it's far away, has a way of getting at you in the end.

Michael was just as he was, gazing into space. But Edith somehow knew he was taking in every word.

– People say soldiering does men good, but I can't see it. To my mind it's the little things that make people brave or cowardly. Besides, what right have we to take another man's life, for no reason other than he's there in the way? You can understand if it's a man's missus attacked by a bunch of hoodlums – but if it's just because someone with more stripes on his arm gives you an order – what right has he, mmm, to tell you to kill? I'm not really that religious, see, but after Albert went I got to thinking more about such things – and right now, lovey, I tell you I'd put my hand on my heart and say it's a mortal sin to take away another man's existence when all that's different between you is the colour of your uniform.

Edith paused, shocked. She had never uttered such a speech, in all her life. Yet now, to a complete stranger – Edith turned and contemplated Michael's sallow face in the lamp-lit gloom.

– What d'you say, then?

Michael slowly turned towards her. The wax-like skin and emaciated features were the same, but there was now a quiet stillness about his eyes which was new. What was it about this face which was so profoundly familiar? Edith suddenly remembered a moment, twelve months before, sitting in a side-chapel near the flower-strewn coffin of her husband. There was a picture across the nave, lit by restless candles. It showed a man with just those same sunken eyes and cheeks. Edith Dockerill suddenly wanted to cry.

– They hurt you so much, lovey, didn't they?

Michael nodded.

– I'm sorry.

The stationmaster's voice rang out over the station. The Cardiff express had arrived. Edith Dockerill rose hurriedly, helped the young man towards the third-class compartments. There, as Michael settled into his seat, Edith went against nature and custom a third time, pressing into the boy's palm the last few coins from her purse

– Get them to find you a cab, when you get to Cardiff. Promise?

Michael stared solemnly at his new friend, nodded. There was an echoey whistle. Doors were slamming all around them. Edith quickly bustled out of the carriage, stood anxiously on the platform as the train began to inch away, with great sighs from its pistons. The woman thought she saw Michael's pale hand, waving, as the train made a bend in the distance, always accelerating. But she might have been mistaken.

An hour later, back in the familiar low-roofed terraces of north Kilburn, Edith Dockerill slipped quietly inside her front-door.

Lights were dim about the house. Glen Miller's *Star Dust* was playing somewhere, on a radio.
– Di – ? I'm home, Di!
Edith crept softly into their small, square front parlour. Somewhere amidst piled clothes-horse and shopping-bag and ironing-board was a slim, dark-haired girl, curled asleep next to the flicker of a gas-fire. Edith smiled to herself, approached, sat down beside her. The woman stroked the hair of her sleeping daughter for some moments. Di's eyes flickered open. She smiled blearily up at her mother.
– Hello mum.
– Hello.
– Did it go off alright?
– What?
– The man and that –
– Oh – yes – I think so, love.
Edith smiled uncertainly. Di yawned. Edith rose, wandering to the front-window. Her back was towards her daughter, now.
– I gave him two pounds three-and-six. Just think of that.
The girl stared. Then she rose, stood next to her mother. Together they contemplated a pale half-moon, rising above complications of chimneys and washing lines.
– Did I do right, d'you think?
– Of course you did, mum.

# *Falling Still*

> The Seventh Station. Our Lord Falls a Second Time.
> "My Jesus, how many Times hast Thou Pardoned me
> And how many Times have I fallen again . . ."

At first Michael ran from room to room, a mad thing. Ivy cottage was small and so a strange procession was made of it, with his bewildered parents stumbling after, still in their night-clothes, bumping into each other as he changed course like dodgem cars at a fair. And all the time there was that scream, regular, animal-like.

– No – no – no – no – no – !

Eventually, after about half-an-hour, exhaustion slowed him down. And finally there he was, shuddering in the crook of the stairs, next to where they used to hang back their mackintoshes on rainy Sunday afternoons. Arthur sat next to him, took one of those filthy, emaciated hands in his, began to cry softly.

– Boy – oh, boy –

Violaceae stood in the kitchen, with the door half-closed between. For some reason she could not now fathom, she held a wet tea-towel to her cheek. It shook uncontrollably. She put it down on the table. She took a weak step, leant on the gas-stove for comfort. Tears, thousands of them, lay in the pit of her stomach, with the weight of a swollen river. Turning, she heard her son's weak moans just a few feet away, accompanied now by the sound of Arthur's fingers, rubbing hectically up and down Michael's back, desperate to bring warmth.

What had happened? Violet's mind went numb at the thought, and suddenly little Anne's face came to her, as she lay inside that ridiculously small coffin on a windy day all those years ago. At this vision, the tears that had lain centuries, came out briefly. She let them. She wept out loud for the first time in many years.

Light intruded vaguely into the house. Somewhere outside a blackbird was pecking noisily at some wet leaves in one of Ivy Cottage's ancient gutters. Everywhere about the dawning garden was the smell, faint, yet achingly sweet, of faraway bluebells in the depths of Penlan Woods. This would soon be a warm Sunday morning in May. The sky would be egg-shell blue, filled with the noise of wheeling larks. But no-one from the house would be there to take notice.

At about six o' clock, Michael finally went to sleep, curled in the angle of the stairs. His parents left him, climbed exhaustedly up to their beds. The couple slept for a few more hours until sunshine was hard and warm on the walls. Then Arthur got up, foraged about the house for a telephone number he had idly scribbled down a month ago, found it at last and called Dr Morris.

An hour later, at about noon, the big black phone rang out in Ash Street, Penclydach. Lilly answered it. She hardly said anything as that strange-sounding brother-in-law's voice babbled on and on, the other end. But when she put the phone down, her face was white as a sheet. An hour later, Violet's younger sister, Bridget, took the slow stopping-train down the Clydach valley, towards the flatlands of Cardiff. All the way, her fingers clung to her patent-leather handbag, and her eyes gazed through and past the view. She was not that pretty, yet her face had an openness which impressed all she met. Now, journeying towards a pain she could not fathom, those gentle features were gripped with fear. She seemed to hear Arthur's words, still, relayed to her in a hoarse whisper by the ghost-like Lilly.

– Someone must come – he might do anything – we just can't cope –

By chance Bridget had been visiting her older sisters from up north where she now lived. Childless yet happily married, she taught at a Yorkshire country primary school where the only disturbance came from wood-pigeons, scuffing at moss-covered tiles of the roof. When the phone-call came that morning, Bridget knew straightaway what she had to do. Who better than someone from right outside? So she brushed aside Lilly's protests and went into the passage for her coat and bag. Before she knew it, she was striding hurriedly down Ash Street towards the railway station, popping a boiled sweet into her mouth for comfort. It was only now, hours later, staring out at shifting patterns of south-Welsh woodland, that Bridget remembered the day, many years before, when Violet had found her at the bottom of Dada's fruit-garden, covered in stings from a wasp's nest, screaming for all she was worth. Mama was nowhere to be found, but Vi was old and big enough to carry her inside. There she bathed her baby-sister's face and arms over and over with bowl-fulls of warm water and bicarbonate of soda, so that gradually the worst of that terrible pain went away. They had cuddled playfully next morning, but had Bridget ever thanked her sister properly? Her form-teacher said later that Violet had probably saved her life, because stings like that can swell up and do all sorts of terrible things.

Bridget gave a sigh, looked down at her fingers, small and precise, clasping the hand-bag for all they were worth. Here, forty years on, was her chance to give something back.

– Be strong, now, girl.

Her voice sounded strange in the empty compartment. She took a deep breath, popped another boiled sweet in her mouth.

Ivy Cottage appeared oddly normal when Bridget finally arrived, just after lunch. Dapples of windy sunshine were scattered about the lawn. There was a smell of young beech leaves and wood-smoke and wall-flowers. Part of her longed to stop right there and drink in all these rich country sensations, but her purpose lay firm about her heart. She strode up to the front-door. As her hand rose to the red-painted knocker, she caught sight of a moon-like face staring out at her through a piece of rippled hallway glass. The door juddered noisily. Violaceae stood there, lips constructing the strangest of smiles.

– Thank you for coming.

They hugged clumsily on the doorstep, leaves rustling about their shoes. Days later, Bridget realised that this was the first time she had been held in her sister arms since the day of the wasps. Now, years on, they parted awkwardly. Bridget was ushered hurriedly within. The unnatural heat from the kitchen hit the younger sister's cheeks. A kettle was burning dry on the gas-stove, long forgotten.

Bridget, suddenly giddy, longed to sit down. But there was a murmuring now from the front-room beyond them, and as she gazed through a narrow gap in the door, she could see a youngish, smartly-dressed man, there in the twilight, bent assiduously over a front-room sofa. Vi was up close, now, whispering in her ear.

– New doctor – came just before you –

Before she could finish there was a strange moaning and mumbling and then a rush of arms and legs in the dimness as a tall, pyjama-clad form lurched out into the kitchen and made for the back-door like some beast from the forest. Bridget's hand went to her mouth, as Geraint Morris appeared with Arthur close on his heels, dashing across the kitchen at lightning speed in a desperate attempt to grapple the creature to the floor before he got out. A high, piteous wail, all the while, rebounding on the damp, shiny walls.

– No, please – no please – no please –

Then, in a moment that Bridget was to remember for the rest of her life, Michael's face finally resolved itself at the kitchen door, in a shaft of early-afternoon May sun. She had been prepared for a painful transformation, but this emaciated mask, quite unlike anything properly human, took her breath away. Despite herself, her eyes made indelible each detail. The sunken, bloodshot eyes. The hollow, wax-like cheeks. The hands, patterned by strange criss-crossing wounds.

In God's name what had happened?

Dr Morris eventually managed to inject a sedative. Michael was returned to the front-room, leaving trails of pale saliva along the way. The four adults finally returned to themselves, sitting in silence at the kitchen table. Only then did Bridget notice that grim odour which lay everywhere about the house. In one corner of the room sat a pile of tattered, urine-soaked clothes, partly covered by an old towel. Bridget wanted to be sick, somehow kept the feeling down. A thin quavering voice broke the quietness at last. It was Arthur.

– What will we do, doctor?

Geraint Morris pursed his lips. This was the first time he had met with such a case in his short career, but it was important always, the London teachers said, to convey an impression of experience.

– The injection will calm his system. Then he'll need to see a specialist. I'll talk to the hospital, first thing, start the ball rolling. Meanwhile, best to get a bit of rest, both of you, mmm? I'll pop in again after tea, to see how things are.

With this, Geraint Morris rose, fingering his trilby. A clock struck the hour somewhere. He looked up from the stone floor, offered each of them a quick, reassuring smile. A good, kind face, Bridget thought to herself, with a pang of hope.

– Ring my wife if you need anything, yes? Don't worry, Zina is used to getting calls.

Arthur rose, gripped the doctor's hand, without a word. Violet bustled across the room to show their guest out. Geraint Morris's hand-stitched London shoes clicked brightly away down the garden path.

– Warmer, now, mmm?

A few hours later, Michael woke with opaque, drugged eyes. Bridget and her sister guided him gently to the bathroom where they bathed him all over with warm water and best toilet-soap. Then they dressed him in fresh clothes, just as if he was a seven-year-old. Finally, after twenty minutes or so manoeuvring him downstairs, they had him sitting on a straight chair in the hall. Here tears sprang suddenly from his eyes and he began to talk rapidly to his dead sister.

Through the rest of that day he continued with this conversation, unwavering, eager and animated. Violet and Arthur were unable to make sense of more than an odd phrase, here and there, amidst the tumult of disconnected words. Yet these muffled, obscure snatches of language were impelled by a passion and yearning which took their breath away. Eventually the three adults trooped out of the hall, made a meal in the kitchen, chatting with embarrassed inconsequentiality as the hubbub went on out there, beyond the door.

What could have happened to the boy?

Bridget stood on Ivy Cottage's doorstep as dusk was finally falling, carrying her folded burberry and bag. The sun had not quite gone, casting ripples of golden light, restless across the smooth grey bark of the beech trees. A shy, blue-tufted jay sat on the well-head coping, cocking its ear curiously towards that continuing mumbling from within the house. Bridget watched Arthur furiously polishing his glasses on the corner of a crumpled handkerchief.

– Well, right then –

Searching for words of comfort, trying desperately to avoid the false and hollow.

– A nice young Doctor. I'm sure he'll know what's for the best. Promise me both you won't worry too much?

Violet stood at the back, hugging the dimness of the house.

– No, we won't –

Bridget breathed in, took a decisive step, pressed kisses on her sister's and brother-in-law's cheeks.

– Give us a ring, mmm? I'll come again, soon.

– Oh, Bridget.

Arthur's bony hand, now, gripping hers as if it would never let go. And the boy's mumbling all the while, drifting from the house, out into the golden dapples. Bridget found herself walking away down the garden path, engulfed almost at once by those dizzy, chokingly sweet, early-summer scents. How can life be so beautiful at a time like this? She turned back at the gate to wave, but they had both gone back inside and the cottage looked as calm as a picture-postcard – but for the humming which mingled now with buzz of an assiduous bumble-bee. Bridget was about to turn back when she noticed the shape of the well-head – and for a brief instant she glimpsed that great plunging darkness her poetical brother-in-law had once told her about, reaching down to the Centre of the Earth.

In God's name what had happened to that poor boy?

Hours later, in the warmth of a fire-lit Ash Street front parlour, Bridget sat next to her sister wondering if it hadn't all been just a terrible dream. Had her nephew really panted like an animal at the kitchen door? Perhaps her exhausted mind was playing tricks! Perhaps it wasn't quite as bad! It was then that she noticed the stains of Michael's spittle everywhere on her dress, and she knew that what she remembered was true.

After a late lunch, Geraint Morris went straight to the hospital. A short conversation with the duty psychiatrist yielded little, but at least procedures had been set in motion and there would be a proper consultant soon on the scene. The doctor returned home. The house was oddly silent. A note on the kitchen table told him that Zina had gone off to church evensong with a neighbour. He carefully put away the photograph and glass and wooden frame that still sat on the carpet. That job would do for another day.

An hour later the doctor returned to Ivy Cottage to check and re-dress Michael's many wounds and abrasions. There was an odd calm in Ivy Cottage kitchen as he worked. Arthur and Vi stood there, as if they had been carrying this burden for years – not hours. When he rose to go, Vi pressed half a yeast cake into his hands.

– Your wife might like a little – for her tea.

The doctor was curiously touched. He wandered off down the lane, thoughtfully. Finally, as darkness was falling, he got back home. Zina was standing in the kitchen, rocking the baby to sleep in her arms. His young wife's long, auburn hair, caught in the richness of the kitchen fire, seemed the most beautiful thing in all the world. He took out his parcel.

– D'you like yeast cake?
– I've never tried it.
– Well, now you shall.

A few minutes later, they sat down for their supper, with the yeast cut up on one of his mother's best porcelain plates. Geraint Morris knew Zina's question was coming, but he said nothing. Finally she murmured:

– Will that boy be alright?
– I think so.
– You don't sound very sure.
– I'm not.
– What will happen to him, Geraint?

The young man paused, listened to that comforting sound of ripples, drifting into the house.

– I remember a professor once saying that the brain is the most healing part of the human body.

Later that night, the young doctor retreated into the darkroom. After an hour Zina knocked politely on the door and joined him in the comforting dark. Her husband's fingers toyed with a fragment of Ilford paper, eddying it beneath waves of developer. They both found themselves leaning forward, watching as an image magically resolved. Pale, weather-worn limestone, voluptuous almost, draped with ivy and fern.

– Was that where we went last week?

He nodded, remembering their Saturday-afternoon ramble through slender Penlan birches, leading suddenly to this strange spot which, he learned later from Mr Champion at the village shop, was once the entrance of an iron-ore working. Strange to think of people going down there, day after day, deep under Penlan hill – even as far back as Roman days, so Mr Champion said.

– Let's go again, this weekend? I'll get Megan to mind the baby.

They grinned at each other, thinking of picnic-baskets and sunny woodland glades. Was it true about that underground lake? The locals called it Blue Water, because once a day in summer a shaft of sun came right down one of the adits to hit the water and make it, for a few short minutes, bright ultramarine. It might be nice, one day, Geraint Morris thought, to do a bit of pot-holing, see for himself.

– What are you thinking about, love?

– Oh – nothing much.

In the silence between them then, came a sound very different from river ripples. A cry, far off, on the edge of their senses. Was it a fox-bark? An owl? Or was it him, maybe? Michael? Both thought it, put the idea hurriedly away.

– I'd better wash up.

– I'll help, love.

– No – it's alright! You've had a full day.

Geraint Morris was alone once more in the darkroom. The room felt colder. He listened. Nothing. Perhaps it had just been their anxious imaginations. Packing away trays and jars and chemicals the young doctor determined to go down into Cardiff sometime soon for a pair of good pot-holing boots. Maybe he could even take his camera down into the caves with him, try out some long-exposures – choose a nice sunny afternoon so he might even see the blue water for himself.

Whilst Geraint Morris was thinking these things, across the valley, Michael was having another fit. This time Violet sat woodenly on a kitchen chair as her husband raced ineffectually from room to room, following their eighteen-year-old son.

– Oooo – oooo – ooo –

Unknown to his parents, Michael was now fleeing from all those burly squaddies, hundreds of them it seemed, who had tormented him in the ROAC Guardhouse, week after week. There they were, chasing him from room to room, brandishing pick-handles and mess-tin lids and shrieking obscenities non-stop at the top of their voices.

– What are you, laddy – ? What are you – !

Finally Arthur managed to trap his son in his arms beside a heaped clothes-horse. There they remained for some minutes, until Michael's breathing began to slow. The young man was some two inches taller than his father at this time in his life, and so the middle-aged man looked upwards at his off-spring, and felt Michael's hot shafts of terror down his cheek. A profound anger was being born. The emotion had probably been there ever since the moment Michael arrived home, but this was the first time Arthur recognised it. He waited for the feeling to abate, but it remained. This kind of rage would stay a long time.

Later that night, Violet heard a commotion upstairs. Arthur was ransacking the bedrooms.

– Whatever are you looking for!

Her husband didn't answer. Instead, a whoop of triumph as he lifted an old Remington out of a debris of old text books and GPO office-journals. Planting the dusty typewriter on his writing desk, Arthur fed in a sheet of best pale-blue Basildon Bond and began hammering furiously, in capitals.

## TO THE MINISTRY OF WAR

Arthur did not send this first letter, filled to ten long pages with the rambling eloquence of a father's pent-up pain. However, others were written, many others – some of which finally found their way into the post-box over the next months and years. Downstairs meanwhile, leaning next to the glowing radiogram, Michael listened to a faraway orchestra playing Brahms' Second Symphony, noticing how that strange metallic clattering from upstairs seemed oddly in time to the beat of the timpani. For a brief instant the compassionate features of an office supervisor in Praed Street came flickering into the boy's imagination and he experienced a moment of quiet rest. Then the soldiers' angry faces returned.

Next morning, Dr Morris arrived at the house to find the young man docile enough to begin a more considered examination. Taking up one of his much-loved red-bound notebooks, the practitioner made a neat list:

*Superficial transverse wounds to back of hands and fingers, some recent, caused by sharp object, probably metallic.*

*Whitlows and other septic spots on arms and legs, origin and cause unknown.*

*Severe weight-loss, features sallow, eyes sunken and bloodshot.*

*Severe anxiety episodes.*

*Fits of delirium, hears voices and speaks to imaginary persons.*

*Irrational desire to run away.*

Before he left that day, Geraint Morris took a leisurely stroll around Ivy Cottage garden with Arthur. The doctor noticed that there seemed to be a new will and tenacity about the man, despite his evident physical and emotional exhaustion. What had changed?

– I phoned Aldershot.

– Ah. Yes. Did they say anything?

Arthur shook his head mechanically. A flurry of wind threw up a few golden beech leaves still on the ground from last year. They sat down on the swing-seat. Together they swung slowly to and fro, feeling the softness of the wind.

– I said, *What's happened to my boy?* They told me he'd been discharged from the Army. That was it. Wouldn't say another word. Said I'd have to write a letter if I wanted any more information.

– Will you?

Arthur turned, stared.

– I want justice. Wouldn't you?

Geraint Morris thought of his beautiful wife and their second unborn child nestling already in her womb, and gazed at this man with new respect. There was silence for some moments, just the quiet squeak of the swing-seat and the hiss of trees. Dr Morris contemplated the dazzling greenery of Penlan wood and suddenly realised with a jolt that here, at Ivy Cottage, they were less than half a mile from the feeder-entrance he had photographed a week before. Were they sitting now above the underground lake?

– He was a good boy, doctor. Got his Matriculation. On his way to a good career.

– I'm sure he was.

Arthur's hands bunched nervously on his lap.

– I've been wondering, though – with all that's happened – will he ever get back to what he was?

Dr Morris looked past Arthur's pebble-lenses, saw the fear and uncertainty in the man's eyes. Those Professors teach you nothing about this kind of thing, he thought.

– We must try to be patient, mmm? Wait for the experts to examine him. They will know what to do.

Arthur got up, stood staring towards the house. Geraint Morris felt the sadness in the man's back, dangling arms, splay of his legs. He tried to put cheerful conviction into his voice.

– I've already arranged a consultation. Michael will see a very experienced psychiatrist, I can assure you. There are so many advances in this area since the war! New chemicals, technical procedures. I'm sure something will be found for the boy –

– Thank you doctor.

There was a flurry of colder air, suddenly all around them. Dr Morris turned up his collar, wondering about home, but then Violaceae was standing there before them, out of the blue, brandishing a huge mug of tea and a chipped plate on which sat two plain ration-book biscuits. Dr Morris could hardly refuse, and so he sat back down, balancing plate and mug on his knee, whilst the woman bent her head close in his ear.

– My worry is – that's he'll go the same way – d'you see?

The young doctor contemplated those lost, lapis lazuli eyes, squeezed between folds of cheaply-powdered flesh. A momentary desolation went through him. Hurriedly recovering himself he attempted a professional smile.

– I suspect that your husband is a lot stronger than you fear.

Violet looked weary and bitter. There was rain in the air, now. Dr Morris quickly consumed the snack and took his leave.

Upstairs in his bedroom, Michael lay curled like a baby, still feeling the blows of a thousand rusty mess-tin lids on his fingers. His hands made tiny convulsive movements, scrubbing at an infinity of Guardroom floors. Each time he had lost consciousness during his imprisonment at Aldershot, Privates Gardner, Bailey and Goodheart seem to have battered his hands with their mess-tins to wake him up again. And then, when he had opened his eyes drunkenly, they had made strange chimpanzee faces and gibbering sounds.

– Loony – loco – cuckoo – !

Once they had said something about his dead sister and Michael had somehow found the strength to crawl across the guardhouse floor near enough to cover Goodheart's tunic with spit. That was the day when they had kicked him to the ground on the verandah in front of three civilian catering-staff, who had been speedily hurried into the distance. After that he was kept in darkness for thirty-six hours, with only lice for company, until the Company Sergeant Major arrived on the scene and he was given something grey and swamp-like and made to eat.

Another day Private Bailey pretended to have a telephone conversation with Michael's bereaved mother.

– Sorry, laddy. The old man's croaked, so she says. Heart conked out. Must have been all that waiting for your letter!

Michael's wild moan mingled with peals of laughter, echoing around the cemented walls. This time Michael went for the shorter man's throat, so that suddenly Private Gardner was screaming for air and the other two had to pin him to the ground and dowse him with the contents of the cell piss-pot before he could calm down.

But now in Ivy Cottage Michael saw Private Gardner again, leering in a dark corner of bedroom and so he made a second lunge, much better than before, and had Gardner good and proper this time, squeezing at the florid redness of his neck until the skin eventually broke and the whole room was drowned in blood. And as Michael saw the world turned crimson he wept there in the hall, feeling the ice-cold of the stone-tiles beneath his feet and glimpsing again all those angel-creatures, seated on the beech-tree branches, like so many rainbow-coloured pigeons. And now, eight-years-old for a second wondrous time, Michael clambered aboard the old balsa-wood Fokker and whizzed out through Ivy Cottage's front-door, past a bewildered Gardner and Bailey and Goodheart, climbing higher and higher into the bright, angel-filled air . . .

Arthur and his wife were just returned inside the house from Dr Morris when they saw their pyjama-clad son, teetering like some ungainly albatross on the outside-ledge of Ivy Cottage's landing-window. Racing headlong into the house, Arthur somehow managed to get a hand to his boy in time, before he threw himself down onto the stone pavings of the garden path some twenty feet below. From that day on, the boy's parents made a point of bolting tight all upstairs windows, as well as removing any sharp or dangerous objects from the house. Then one night, just a week after Michael's return, Arthur woke in a cold sweat in the early hours, tore downstairs in his night-clothes and out into the moonlit garden. Dragging a heavy lump of Penlan sandstone right across the lawn from the rockery he finally managed to tilt it over the mouth of the well-entrance, covering it forever.

You never know.

# Comforters

*The Eighth Station. The Women of Jerusalem Mourn Him.*
*"My Jesus, Laden with Sorrows!*
*I weep for the Offences I have Committed against Thee . . ."*

Geraint Morris made arrangements for Michael to be admitted into Heol Llyn hospital just a few weeks after his return from Aldershot, at the end of May, 1948. Following an obscure impulse, the doctor took the boy's photograph on Ivy Cottage lawn the day before he went for his first consultation. Swimming into focus in the developing-bath, the young man's image was revealing in unexpected ways. Those oddly-angled, bony shoulders. Those lorry-tyre crossed legs. Those tragi-comic, elephantine ears. Finally, Michael's eyes which seemed so defiantly lapis-lazuli, despite the black-and-white. A kind of innocence remained there, the doctor mused, which nothing could blot out.

Heol Llyn's admission-report revealed a somewhat more objective view of the case:

*A pale young man of typically asthenic appearance. During the interview he was not uncooperative, but his manner was vague, detached and in keeping with a general facial apathy. He gave at first a scrappy history and his replies to questions, though to the point, were predominantly monosyllabic. He complained of 'bad nerves', difficulties with concentration, and 'no will to do anything'. Diagnosis: schizophrenia.*

Sitting on a straight-backed chair, facing into a shaft of warm spring sunshine proceeding from the clinician's half-open office-window, Michael made shapes with his long fingers, following the whorls of the wood-grain beneath his seat. Occasionally he would commence a faint, tuneless whistling, then would smile momentarily at nothing in particular – before finally relapsing into his former, dormant state.

Professor Gilbert surveyed his new patient in silence. He was in no hurry, understanding from long experience that the soul's secrets are not to be rushed out all at once, for the world's convenience. His first questions were therefore careful, tentative, keeping to the outward facts. In this way Michael's story emerged, fragment by fragment, portions of which Gilbert noted down later for the file, in a neat, flowing hand. Though the consultant psychiatrist did not know it at the time, this narrative differed in several crucial respects from that recorded in the army's confidential reports:

*Asked by his Sergeant Major why he would not drill, Michael replied that he could not do anything when he was being shouted at. He was then put on a charge and confined to the guardhouse. He was determined to run away, however, and somehow broke free. He got as far as Aldershot station, but was there arrested by military police, after which he was given a further fourteen days detention. From now on it seems his life was a crescendo of misery, with long periods of solitary confinement in the guardhouse. He was made to scrub floors. When he fainted from exhaustion, he was immediately woken up and told to carry on, as before. He was forced to lie on the stone floor for hours on end. If he tried to get up, he was beaten by guards. They taunted him frequently, saying things like: 'Look at his eyes! You can see he's crazy!' They pretended to phone his parents. They told him that he had talked in his sleep and confessed everything. One day he could stand no more. He had a fight with one of his guards, during which he was injured about the eye, and had to be treated at Cambridge Military Hospital. On his return his imprisonment continued with increasing amounts of physical cruelty. If he stopped working, or disobeyed an order, he was beaten across the fingers with mess-tin lids. He was not allowed to wash, or be hygienic in his habits. Finally he lost track of time, day or night, and considered that life would never change. After some indefinable period (no more than a month), he appeared before an Army Medical Board and was invalided. A few days before his final discharge he was cleaned up and dressed in new clothes.*

James Gilbert was a figure of unusually large dimension, who invariably caused a stir of eager activity amongst the nurses when he came onto the ward. He was a popular man with everyone, yet his easy smile and twinkling eyes hid a ruthless ambition. The source of this is not hard to find, for, in this early post-war period, Gilbert was one of a new generation of professionals, determined to free psychiatry from centuries of myth and superstition and ally it at last with the rigours of twentieth-century science.

Gazing up from his neatly stacked files, the professor contemplated the stiffly polite forms of Arthur and Violet later that morning with the usual pang of compassion. This was the first time they had met and the doctor considered some words of tender solicitude. He put the idea away, however. Professionalism dictated that he commence with the clinical picture. And so he began his account of the case in soft, measured tones. They listened quietly enough. Nevertheless, Gilbert sensed that there was much in what he said which was new and hard for them both to take in. As in so many instances, he reflected, the ordinary man or woman has little or no understanding of the mysteries of psychological breakdown.

Gilbert finished at last, made an cathedral-arch of his fingers in a pool of that spring sunshine which now bathed whole swathes of his spacious room. The wife, he noticed, was staring fixedly at a piece of green radiator-piping. The husband, bent over like a supplicant. The poor man's Adam's apple rose up and down painfully. An agreeable warmth spread within as Gilbert prepared to offer at last the gift of his profession.

– Now, as to the all-important issue of treatment. I don't suppose you have heard of Deep Insulin therapy?

Their faces swivelled in unison, engaged him in the blankest of stares. He smiled gently, offering that look of kindly omniscience which his nurses loved best.

– No need for any worries. The procedure is new, but both simple and efficacious, especially in cases of affective disorder, such as your son.

Their nods, again in perfect unison. The sun had found them now, he saw, wreathing their expectant forms in two crowns of gold.

– I can explain all the details when we meet next for the first session. I have pencilled Monday morning, if that's alright? It's best not to waste too much time. Our rosta normally starts at ten. Shall we say nine-thirty, then, here in my office?

With that Professor Gilbert rose hugely, offering each of his visitors the firm, sweet-smelling warmth of his hand.

That night at around seven, Violaceae briskly walked up the mountain road to be in good time for her weekly whist-drive. Arthur's face registered a flicker of surprise at her announcement just after dinner, but he did not demur. If asked he would have admitted that he too wanted to be alone. And so now, as daylight imperceptibly faded, she made her way through lemonish arches of beech and sycamore towards that squat Nissen hut where the women would already be gathering loudly. What would she say if they asked?

Nothing. Say nothing at all.

Then, as the last scent of heavy-headed bluebells filled her senses, she found herself remembering for no reason the very first day when Michael had come into the world. So many years ago, it seemed to be part of another life. Yet the pain of the labour, she remembered that! And the joy of knowing that now, after so many quiet months of waiting, it would soon be over and she would bring forth in purest mystery all that she ever wanted in this world – the eager helplessness of infant life. And then, on that icy Christmas morning in 1929, her young husband had appeared with a half-tipped cup of weak tea and even in the sharp finality of her labour she loved the tender solicitude in his bright eyes which reminded her of the dark indigo of Penclydach wood where his lips had first touched the ardent expectancy of her cheek.

Later, when Michael had first nipped at her breast his tiny mouth seemed to take possession of her soul. And yet then, yes, even then in those first simple days, there was a warning somewhere inside. Things were good, very good – but she was sure to be punished. You don't have to be chapel-born to know that no-one gets happiness at such a low price! And so for a little while she lived in the shadow of uncertainty. Then precious little Annie came into the world and her heart opened up like a flower, banishing at a stroke all her doubts and fears.

But it was Annie, her favourite, her joy and her blessing – who was snatched out of life by a vengeful God, on a day which stayed with her like a hot brand, burning and scarring all that ever was. Violaceae's flesh, shorn of happiness and peace, grew flaccid. Her lapis lazuli eyes lost light and life. Just dull, mechanical purpose now – and a bitten-down anger which sometimes, as now, longed for her son's speedy end. Then at least they could have done with the lot of it!

– Or me. I should die. After all, it was me that let Annie go out onto that road.

Now, as the warm lights of the Nissen hut rose up before her, Violet paused in her stride, smiling bitterly up at the black heavens. God knew she wouldn't end her life! She had too much of Dada's religion for that. Yet still, for a brief moment, the woman savoured the thought of it, punishing her better than anything and taking away all the terrible pain.

– Your deal, Vi!

Their faces, her neighbours, welcoming, full of easy comradeship. Violet could not disappoint them. She dealt, her hands already moist with the yellow warmth of the room. And the game, as usual, took hold of her. Indeed she played rather well that night, winning hand after hand, just as if Michael and Aldershot and Deep Insulin did not exist.

A mile down the road, meanwhile, in a dim Ivy Cottage bedroom, Arthur stared down at a typewritten page:

*This letter is to inform you that I shall be writing forthwith to the Minister of War, urging him to order an Inquiry into the full facts of this case. No financial consideration can begin to compensate for the suffering and serious harm caused to my son, but I can assure you that I shall be demanding nonetheless –*

The typewriter key had stuck on the second s, jamming the mechanism. Arthur tore the sheet out of the roller, crushed it angrily between his fingers, began anew –

*This letter is to give you formal warning that I shall be –*

An owl hooted sadly somewhere up in Penlan wood. Arthur

paused for inspiration. How silent the house now seemed after all the moaning and humming! He seemed to see his son, then, in his mind's eye, standing next to the garden well, dressed in a pair of striped mental-hospital pyjamas. Beside him on the grass, a broken bicycle, one of its wheels still spinning. And there, along the garden path, a trail of bloodstains, just like those left in the snow last Christmas by that poor wounded fox.

Two weeks before, Michael had taken his bike from the shed in the early hours of the morning and raced off in pitch blackness, pedalling madly north towards his aunts in Penclydach. He got a few miles before plunging down an embankment. The police found him, returning him to the house shortly before dawn, along with the remains of the bike, strapped to the back of a local delivery-van. The very next night, Michael tried again, this time stealing a child-sized cycle from a neighbour. The tyres were flat. He crashed into a tree after less than a mile, this time returning up the garden path alongside a local constable, leaving that trail of red behind. After that, everyone in the village was told to lock their sheds at night.

*I swear to you in all solemnity –*

Arthur found himself longing for his son, now, even in all his mad raving. The thought of that cold hospital ward where Michael lay cut the man to the quick. What was this strange thing called Deep Insulin? Arthur put the question hurriedly away. There would be plenty of time for that next week. Poising two fingers tremulously above the Remington, his brows knit in a concentrated furrow, creating a tiny dark line which would, in the months to come, divide his aging temples into two equal halves, stigmata of all that fought against itself within.

*I shall dedicate my whole life*

Seven miles away Michael lay in the rustling twilight of Blethyn Ward, staring calmly up at the ceiling. There were several Amazon-like cracks there, the shapes of which he had been following assiduously, over and over, as the hours of night were played out. Since telling his story to that nice professor, his mind had been somehow eased. And although they came up, Goodheart and Bailey and the rest, nudging and grinning, he no longer broke into a cold sweat every time they were near. He felt somehow protected. It was as if the professor's words covered him like a blanket. Outside this, life drifted on, murmuring, half-lit, inconsequential. Inside the blanket was Michael and his curled-up thoughts and feelings: safe, secure, and mysteriously softened. It was all thanks to the professor, Michael knew, and to the nurses, and to the sodium amytal which they fed him now four times a day.

Annie had gone too – and it was a bit of a relief, he had to admit. Having her sitting next to him every moment of the day had been a little too much in the end. Just before she went off, he had shrieked at her, he remembered, losing all of his stammer and the awful twitching of his eye. She looked so shocked! Her lips trembled. Her eyes filled with big baby-tears. He had never seen her blubber like that before and he was rather pleased at his achievement. Finally she scooted off, leaving a trail of broken dandelion-heads. He was not sorry. Was she back at the bottom of the well where she used to live? Or maybe she was hiding in that dark limestone cave up in Penlan wood. Of course she would come back, he knew, in time. Meanwhile, though, life would be easier. And even as he thought this, he saw before him the bowl of thin porridge on the ward breakfast-trolley, with its lump of raspberry jam at the centre. Would it be as soft and sweet and yesterday's? He was sure it would.

Michael had first heard the word insulin at school. It was not like porridge and jam but it sounded simple and wholesome, all the same. Would it take all the voices away? Would it see off Goodheart and his angry grin? Would it rid him of all the flushes and tremblings and twitchings which had bedevilled him since the beginning of time? Things could be so different! And suddenly, as if re-discovering a simple life before the Fall, Michael saw himself back there, calmly ascending Ivy Cottage's fourteen stairs, balancing two cups of Hornimans on a tray, twin offerings to those who first brought him to this life.

Michael closed his eyes on this beatific thought, feeling sleep coming at last, soft as the wing-beat of a Penlan owl.

Deep Insulin or Coma Therapy, (so Professor Gilbert's latest Lancet article stated), was first developed by Sakel at Potzl's clinic in Vienna in the late-thirties. Working with drug addicts, Sakel discovered that insulin injections had the effect of reducing dramatically that restlessness and irritation with invariably follows withdrawal from the object of addiction. Encouraged, he began to experiment on a wider range of patients, notably the more intractable cases of dementia praecox – or schizophrenia as it was now fashionably called. Sakel quickly discovered that progressive injections of insulin would produce in all but the most resistant patients a hypoglycaemic, or deep-coma state, which, if sustained for periods of up to an hour-and-a-half, resulted in a marked diminution in even the severest of their symptoms.

With the War came a dramatic rise in anxiety-neurosis and shell-shock, giving fresh impetus to Sakel's researches. A methodology of insulin treatment was being refined which could be soon applied clinically by therapeutic teams working on psychiatric wards throughout the Allied Territories. It was modern armed conflict therefore, James Gilbert's paper argued, which had paradoxically given the medical community the perfect range of clinical experience. And, although there were occasional adverse reactions, and, in a very small percentage of cases, instances of irreversible coma or even mortality – deep-insulin was beginning to prove its worth.

With the end of the War came a further influx of disorders, as soldiers returned to the vicissitudes of civilian life. Coma-therapy continued to thrive in these circumstances, so that by the end of the forties, it was the favoured treatment in almost every mental hospital in the land.

*And I am proud to state, in conclusion, that*
*our efforts are already offering exciting results here in Wales*

Professor Gilbert was flushed with success, but experience taught him to take all the usual precautions. Patients selected for Deep Insulin should be free of serious organic disease. The man or woman was prepared for treatment, laid upon a special high-standing bed, using restraints where appropriate. Injections began normally with a starting-dose of twenty units. Ampoules of glucose, cardiazol, lobeline and caffeine were kept standing by to reverse the procedure if necessary at any time. The following were normally observed by Gilbert and his colleagues during the first few minutes of insulin administration:

- *Sweating, flushing of the face.*
- *Increased salivation, sensations of hunger and thirst.*
- *Mild euphoria (occasionally, wild excitement).*
- *Tremors, clonic twitches.*

Later, the following might be observed:

- *Loss of speech.*
- *Hypertonias.*
- *Pupils dilated, loss of reflexes.*
- *Loss of consciousness.*
- *Fall in body temperature.*
- *Deep coma.*

The hypoglycaemic state was allowed to subsist for no more than ninety minutes, according to the professor's guidelines. At this time the effect of the insulin might be reversed by the passing of a nasal tube and the feeding therein of up to 500cc of sweetened tea. If any adverse reactions were observed, for example convulsions or fits, then the coma-state was to be speedily reversed by the use of intravenous glucose. Some clinicians favoured the encouragement of epileptic fits during coma, on the grounds that this also had a therapeutic effect. However the benefits of this latter approach had not yet been fully proven. A sober scientist first and last, Gilbert never tried it.

Besides, the professor had enough to think about. Coma-therapy might seem simple on the pharmaceutical side, but the clinical progress of each patient needed constant attention. Furthermore, insulin-induced coma-states needed to be repeated at least several times a week, over a period of up to three months. It might also be necessary to increase the dosage over time to sustain frequency of the coma. This was because resistance to insulin could often build up within the body; and it was vital in all cases that a high number of comas be achieved. Indeed, most clinicians, including Gilbert, found that the higher the number of comas, the greater the impact upon the worst symptoms of schizophrenia. Whether this amounted to a cure of this terrible disease remained a matter of debate, however the ameliorative effect upon a large number of sufferers, Gilbert concluded in his Lancet article, *could not be underestimated*.

Twenty-four hours before his first insulin treatment, on the morning of June 20th 1948, Michael was given a full medical examination:

*Blood pressure, 130/80. Urine, reaction acid, specific gravity 1018. Albumen nil, sugar nil. Wasserman reaction, negative. Fundi, normal. No tremors of outstretched hands. Cardio-vascular system, respiratory system, alimentary system: nil abnormal detected. Appetite good. Bowels regular. Bladder satisfactory. Sleeps well.*

Next morning, prompt at a quarter-past-nine, the patient was taken up to Caradoc (the Insulin Ward) where he was given his first injection, according to the rosta, at 9.30am. This first dose, like many others which were to follow, produced no coma. Michael was, it seems, an extremely resistant patient.

Arthur and Violet took the village bus down to Heol Llyn early that same morning. It was a grey, lowering day, without a breath of wind. Inside the bus, most of the seats were empty and Arthur remembered for years after how it seemed to jolt on every bump along the way. They finally stopped not far from a set of high wrought-iron gates. The couple alighted, and, following-out Vi's careful plan, made a show of sauntering off towards a line of nearby shops. As soon as the bus had disappeared from view, however, they returned to the hospital gates and entered.

Caradoc Ward was spacious, newly white-painted and full of strange partitions. Young interns wandered here and there with weird-looking apparatus. There was a smell of ether and body-odour and something else which was heavy and sickly, making Arthur swallow uncomfortably. From nowhere, James Gilbert's hand gripped his.

– Found your way here alright, then?

A friendly glint of the professor's horn-rimmed spectacles. Arthur tried to feel reassured. They rounded one of the partition walls. There he was, lying under a thin cotton sheet, on a bed which seemed very high up from the ground. It was less than a day since they had last seen him, yet Michael looked suddenly so thin and frail. A badly-shaven face lolled towards them, grinned toothily. Eyes rolled, showing their whites. A dribble of divers fluids hung there, on the end of his chin where the nurse had forgot to wipe.

– We gave him his first units earlier on. No coma, this time, I'm afraid, but we're very pleased with your son, all the same.

Arthur felt a wad of anger suddenly there at his throat.

– You said we'd meet first – you said everything would be explained first –

– Did I? Forgive me. We have to start early for a variety of reasons, the nurses' change-overs and so forth.

Professor Gilbert smiled, spread his huge hands, as if to bless them both.

– But as you see – a most encouraging beginning!

Arthur watched himself nod, smile back, thank the professor politely. Satisfied, Gilbert wandered away, beckoning the ward-sister towards another case. Arthur approached Michael's bed. As he leant tenderly over him, he noticed the leather straps and buckles which had been discreetly tucked under the mattress. Arthur embraced his nineteen-year-old son. It was like clutching eggshells. If his arms clung too tight, the boy might be crushed out of existence. Michael's lips were making odd slippery sounds, not at all like words. Arthur let go at last. Violet would want her turn. But where was she? Arthur turned, saw that his wife had wandered right across the ward, hugging the shadows, fiddling with the belt of her coat.

– She can't. Of course. Never mind.

It was drizzling as they emerged into Heol Llyn's spacious grounds half-an-hour later. Arthur had asked his wife to make a thermos and sandwiches just in case. Despite the rain, they sat on a bench next to a line of French poplars, black sticks, rising into the grey. For a few moments they just sat there, in dull silence, feeling the cool of the fine rain on their cheeks. A mangy-looking terrier limped into view from the long grass under the trees. It came up, sniffed at their legs, then at their laps where the sandwiches were, still packed in their grease-proof paper. Arthur took out a luncheon-meat sandwich, popped it into the dog's wide, panting mouth.

– What did you do that for!

Arthur smiled weakly back at his wife. Her furious face turned away, stared up into the nebulous rain. The terrier loped off after a while, licking its jaws. The drizzle was getting thicker all the time. Still they did not move. Arthur uncorked the thermos, carefully removed a rim of sodden newspaper, poured two measures into picnic cups. The tea tasted old, sweet, reassuring. Just like that stuff they gave Michael to wake him up? The man and the woman sipped in unison, both thinking the same thought. Finally, just when Arthur was packing the thermos away, Violaceae spoke. Her voice was oddly gentle.

– All over, then.

– What d'you mean, love?

– You know well enough.

Arthur took off his spectacles, began to rub busily at their misted lenses. Violet watched, breathed a sigh, heavy as the ages.

– I knew it would be like this.

– What d'you mean?

– Don't be so bloody stupid! How else was it going to be? It's over, I tell you. We won't know him. He'll be a stranger in the house.

Arthur balanced his spectacles carefully back on his nose. The rain covered them, almost immediately, just as it had done before.

– Don't, Vi, please don't –

Violaceae turned, looked at her husband, experienced that old, mad desire to pull those stupid glasses off his face and stamp them into a thousand pieces. Instead, she drank the last tepid dregs of her tea, rose, wandered away towards the hospital gates, enveloped in wraiths of mist.

– Come on.

Arthur hurriedly came to himself, packed away what was left of the picnic, stumbled after his wife. Reaching her at last and putting a timid arm under hers, he felt his tears come, thankfully lost in a welter of raindrops. They reached the bus-stop.

– Shall we – you know – stand over by the shops?

She stared at him blank. Then a bitter smile spread across the loose folds of her face.

– It doesn't matter what people think now, does it?

When they got home a long brown envelope had arrived on their hall-carpet. Arthur took it upstairs while his wife bustled about the house.

*From the Ministry of Pensions, Norcross, Blackpool, Lancs, with reference to your recent application for a disability war-pension on behalf of your son*

Arthur's eye travelled down a mass of heavy, smudged typing, until he reached a small paragraph at the bottom of the page.

*Claim rejected. Disability cannot be attributed to Private 22027623's period of service, nor can it have been aggravated thereby.*

A voice, shouting out, muffled from downstairs:

– What was it, Arthur?

Arthur re-folded the letter, placed it carefully in the back of his desk-drawer.

– Nothing, love. Just an acknowledgement, that's all.

That night Arthur had a strange and vivid dream. He was back there, with his school-pals in Penclydach, fishing for tiddlers. As they sat together on a dead log next to the stream, swinging their legs, little Billy danced up, pointing his finger.

– Look! See? There!

Arthur rose excitedly, wading out into the green water. Currents tugged at his skinny young legs as he reached the deepest part. He looked down. There, amidst a forest of swirling weed, was a mermaid-like face.

Oh, God. Annie.

His dead daughter smiled up at Arthur from the depths. So calm and mysterious. How sweet and soft she looked! How alive! Arthur leant forward, touched the surface of the stream, feeling a violent surge of joy.

The forty-year-old man woke with inexplicable happiness still at his throat. For a while he just lay in the darkness next to his sleeping wife, hearing her slow breathing like waves of the sea. A piece of moonlight crossed the wall, finally arrived on her cheek, making her look unexpectedly young.

Next morning, Arthur received another official-looking letter, this time marked *House of Commons*. Again he took it upstairs to his room, to read.

> *I am writing to inform you that I have today arranged for a meeting with Mr Shinwell, at which time I shall press for a full Inquiry into your son's unfortunate experience.*

At the bottom of the page a large flourish of a signature, in royal blue.

*George Price-Richards, MP.*

Later, over breakfast, Arthur told his wife to ring the General Post Office and say he was taken sick. Violet was astonished, but something about her husband's face made her comply without a word. At eleven, pegging out washing in the garden she heard a swirl of Brahms from one of Ivy Cottage's downstairs windows. Her husband was playing Michael's favourite record, over and over.

After lunch, Arthur packed a small satchel and walked up to the top of Penlan hill. There he found a quiet fold of brackened hillside, where the soft June sunshine was the warmest. Stretching out, he shut his eyes drowsily, praying that the dream of Annie in the stream would come back. It didn't of course. But the man woke an hour later, profoundly refreshed. Gazing out across the wooded hills towards the Bristol Channel he fancied he could see that huddle of redbrick buildings and poplar trees which was Heol Llyn. Had they given Michael his second dose of insulin yet? Thirty units, today, the professor had said, to be sure. Would poor Michael survive it all? Or would they have to learn to live with a stranger in the house, as Vi had said? Then Arthur remembered the letter with House of Commons at the top and a swirl of hope and determination went through him. No-one would destroy his son. No-one. Suddenly Arthur saw, in a vision, huge Remington-typing emblazoned across the Basildon-Bond blue of the sky.

*For He was Born on Christmas Day*

The man's heart leapt like a deer.

## Still Falling

*The Ninth Station. Our Lord Falls a Third Time.*
*"My outraged Jesus,*
*By the Merits of the Weakness Thou didst suffer,*
*Give me Strength to Conquer my Wicked Passions . . ."*

A few months later, Michael returned to Ivy Cottage with his father, the young man's tall frame bent and softened by countless futile insulin injections.

They paused at the narrow wicket gate, blinked up together as a cool October air was suddenly filled with dark blizzards of beech. One dry leaf fell upon the smooth dubbin of Michael's shoe. He bent somnolently, plucked it up with those long, piano-playing fingers, studied each vein profoundly. Arthur made an encouraging push. A child-like moan came out of nowhere. The father's hand fell automatically to his side.

– That's alright, boy. You stay there as long as you want.

Violet stood beside the back door, waiting. She had put on weight since her son's return from Aldershot five months ago. Last year's clothes held her now in a demeaning grip, and her chalky face had acquired an odd slant, like a half-subsided wall. Her hands were clenched tight as she waited for Arthur and Michael to arrive. How long had those fingers gripped like that? Minutes? Days? Weeks? She stepped back, shoved the door wide for the two men. Michael did not seem to notice his mother, shuffling into the gloom of the house. The woman experienced a wave of resentment – then giddy relief. Arthur followed his son. His eyes flicked towards his wife, flicked hurriedly away.

On the kitchen table was a tray of bright tea-things, prepared several hours before. A greasy kettle hissed merrily over the gas.

There was a smell of washed sheets and scouring powder. Michael sniffed at these curiously, sitting down obediently before his cup. Arthur poured boiling water into the pot. Violet bustled with biscuit-tin and plates. There were odd, half-articulated sounds between them, scarcely words. Finally the family were set there around the yellow oilcloth, just as in the olden days. Vi poured. Michael's hand went automatically forward for his cup.

– Let it cool off a bit, eh?

The boy's fingers stopped mid-air, hovering obediently at his father's gentle admonition. Arthur glanced furtively towards his wife, poured a puddle of brown onto his son's saucer, held it up for him to sip. Violaceae turned angrily away. Outside, as in a silent film, falling beech leaves drifted through the misty blue of the October sky. Her eyes gazed at all this, did not see . . . Michael's voluptuous lips, meanwhile, approached the pitted edge of the saucer. An inch away they suddenly stopped. A deep, piteous look above the kitchen mantelpiece, where a crack in the masonry made a river's course, not unlike that Amazon written upon a hospital wall. Michael's hands began to make juddering movements in the air, a cryptic semaphore. Arthur tried to pull the saucer back. Too late. A wild pounce at something invisible to normal eyes. Hot brown Hornimans sailed through the air, covering all.

Violet gave a moan, rushed out of the room. Feet stumbled upstairs. A bedroom door slammed furiously.

– Never mind, Michael.

Michael nodded sagely at his father's words. The house lapsed into silence. Just the quiet drip of spilt tea onto the linoleum, mixed with the hiss of leaf-filled breezes outside.

That night Michael swallowed the usual dose of sodium amytal, snuggled down into his old, narrow bed and listened curiously. Was that Anne's distant voice? No. Just the creaking of a beech branch. He wondered then about that deep well-shaft, just a few short feet away, in Ivy Cottage garden. Would she be living down there, still? Or was she gone forever? In that dulled, emollient place which was Michael's mind, such questions could be asked now without great pain. Little terrified him these days, not even the jeering faces of Bailey or Goodheart. And they came very seldom, thin parchment ghosts, more comical than terrifying. One day, a week or so ago, he had even poked out a tongue at them as they sidled up to his hospital bed. That made them run off pretty quick! Michael grinned to himself in the dark at the memory. How easy it all was now, having to feel so little! Professor Gilbert had been right after all when he had chatted at his bed-side on that final day of treatment, covering a grateful patient's shoulder with the huge, fatherly warmth of his hand.

– No need to feel anything you don't want to, eh, lad?

Michael turned onto his side at this last sweet memory, let sleep drift up with cunning invisibility, as it would.

Downstairs, alone in the gloom of a dying front-room fire, Arthur opened a much-creased General Post Office file and poured a pile of official-looking letters onto the carpet. Stern letter-heads loomed, stained with anxious sweat. *Ministry of War. British Legion. Ministry of Pensions. House of Commons.* The correspondence was certainly piling up! Taking a fresh page from his writing-pad, Arthur licked a pencil, began to fashion a new draft for tomorrow morning's hour at the typewriter.

*Dear Sir,*
*It is now all too clear that my son's life will be*
*irretrievably blighted . . .*

In her room, meanwhile, Violaceae undressed as usual, folding each article of clothing in precise order over Mama's old rocker. Approaching the bed in her night-dress, she caught sight of a lumpish paleness in the mirror. For a moment her mind went blank. Who was that intruder? Could that really be her? The woman sat heavily on the counterpane, gazed gloomily at all those distended contours. Where was that slim young girl now, with her triumphant lapis lazuli eyes? A pad of slippered feet on the stairs. Arthur. Passion was long gone. Love, too. What did they have left to feel? Just Michael. He was all that was left. Despite herself, Violaceae was glad the boy was back. Arthur opened the door, smiled hesitantly.

– I made a hot-water-bottle.

Violet nodded, pulled back the sheets.

Winter and spring came and went. Life acquired a semblance of its old normality. Michael was quiet enough, wandering aimlessly about the house, leaving a trail of tuneless humming behind. The sodium amytal gave his face a loose opacity. Sometimes Arthur put a record on and he would sit next to the gramophone, his arms waving in time to the music. But he never went near the well. Pounding out another letter to London, Arthur would sometimes pause, listen for his son's shuffling step on the stairs. Then, occasionally, a terrible need would come upon him to see that other Michael, the first one, the young boy who had pedalled joyously down the lane on his brand-new bike. Yet of course it was impossible, he knew now. That Michael was gone forever.

One day Arthur went back to the hospital and shrieked out at Professor Gilbert standing there in the ward, amid a circle of nurses.

– You promised – you lied to me – you never really cared – !

James Gilbert made a strange shape with his lips, swallowed, strode hurriedly away.

Some time later, Arthur and Violet took their tall, gangling man-child on the train up to Penclydach. A ring of nervously smiling aunts' faces awaited him. By this time, Lilly was married and raising a robust toddler. It was little Archie's duty at this important ceremonial moment to walk across acres of sitting-room pile, offering their visitor a chocolate from a hugely expensive Luxury Selection. This proved no simple task for the child, confused not a little by the strange, tuneless humming which seemed to proceed constantly now from the twenty-year-old's womanish lips.

A tense expectancy. Archie strode manfully across the room, watched by an audience of encouraging faces. Finally he stood before that swaying, sky-scraperish form, waving a chocolate-map with childish urgency. A pale, moon-like face peered down at last, smiled faintly at nothing in particular. Slender, piano-playing fingers descended to forage briefly amongst coloured cellophane and silver paper before plucking out the only strawberry-cream.

Sod him!

It was Archie's favourite. The child tore back across the room, flushed with anger, sat sulkily in the dusk of a curtained window. Michael hardly noticed the infant rage however, calmly popping the strawberry cream between his lips and munching it noisily down. The rest of the world looked on, relieved. No dribbling, no spitting out onto the new carpet! In fact it had gone pretty well, all things considered. As Arthur wandered down to the station an hour later with his church-steeple-like charge, he recalled all that loud talk at the doorstep about future dinners and teas for Michael and his parents. But he and Vi both knew in their hearts: Michael would probably never be visiting there again.

Summer was coming in that Coronation year of nineteen-fifty-three when Violaceae discovered a pain in her stomach which wasn't unwept tears and would never quite go away.

Geraint Morris was called to the house for the first time in many months. The doctor and his wife had three children of their own by now – and despite those hints of foreign exoticism which stubbornly remained, the pair were a solid part of the community. Indeed life was blossoming for a young local practitioner who today ran the largest and most successful practice in the district. Yet now, as Geraint Morris walked up the garden path, he experienced a sinking feeling, formed out of the memory of that terrible day in May 1948 and the farce of all the stupid insulin treatment which followed. He should never have been taken in by Gilbert and his kind! Charlatans and pseudo-scientists! Didn't he learn anything up in London?

But there was also a deeper uneasiness inside him, which was the knowledge that there was probably never going to be a cure for what the boy had. All you could do was calm down the outside. God alone knew what went on within. As he considered these things, Geraint Morris found himself at the door. Over there was the swing-seat, hardly used these days, its paint-work cracked and pealing. Further across the garden, that lump of Penlan stone, patterned now with moss and lichen, covering what was once the well.

Arthur's face, bobbing up, making a show of busy cheerfulness.

– She'll be so glad to see, you doctor.

It was cancer, of course. The illness had been creeping up, the doctor concluded, for quite a time. Far too late for remedies. Back home with Zina, the doctor busied himself with his weekly accounts, but he couldn't get the image of the old woman out of his mind.

– What is it Geraint?

– His wife. Those eyes, looking up at me from the bed. They've all been through so much – but with Violet – you know I don't think she's ever quite faced up. If she had, then maybe it wouldn't have come along –

– The illness?

Geraint hesitated. Then he shook his head firmly. It mustn't be that! After all, the doctor thought, what kind of God would it be who punished people twice for their misfortunes?

As mid-summer approached Violaceae could scarcely leave her bed, buttressing herself against pain like a fortress under siege. Fires burned night and day, blankets piled up, everywhere a clutter of pills and potions and creams. Then, out of the blue, came a change. Entering her room one morning balancing a tray of bread-fingers and Heinz tomato-soup, Arthur was stunned to find the curtains pulled back. He approached the bed, now swathed in bands of dizzy sunshine. Violet's grey, mottled skin was just the same, as was that faint odour of decay. But his wife's face on the pillow was lit with something Arthur had not seen in thirty years.

– What is it?

The man hardly recognised the softness of his sick wife's voice. He put the tray down in a dream, sat on the bed, took Violet's hand in his. Neither spoke. They didn't need to. Arthur felt his wife's fingers pressing into his palm and he was taken back in a leap to that wedding day afternoon when they had raced hand in hand to the railway station, in the pouring rain.

– Why are you smiling, Vi?

– Nothing. I'm not going to fight any more, that's all.

Later Michael shuffled into the room in the slippers he now wore all through the day. Years of tranquillising agents had given his body a sleepwalker's gait; and his eyes were possessed of a drooped emptiness reminiscent of a grazing cow.

Mother and son contemplated each other. It was the first time Violet had met Michael's gaze in a long time.

– Hello, son.

Michael stared. Still his mother's eyes did not go away. The young man's hands began to make odd fluttering movements, a scaled-down version of that wild animation which used to accompany the worst of the hallucinations. Arthur came up. A hand on his boy's shoulder.

– Come along, now, mmm? Let's go down and make some dinner.

At the turn of the stairs, Michael stopped short and his hands began to make that miniature dance again. Arthur gazed at the boy, perplexed. But already Michael's lips were making warbling sounds, archaic beginnings.

– Mmm – what's that? Come again?

– A – ie –

– Yes?

– An – nie –

It was as if a light came to his father. Of course. That was it. The boy knew better than any of them! Looking towards the bedroom he seemed to see Violaceae's transformed face once more. And he understood now how it was indeed his lost daughter who had come strangely alive in the sick woman's blue eyes.

A dribble of tears made a dark patch on Arthur's sleeve. The man patted his weeping man-child comfortingly, nudging him forward, down the rest of the stairs.

– You're right, son. It was little Annie. It really was.

A week later Geraint Morris strolled up Ivy Cottage's garden path, as usual, breathing in deeply to get the best of that wonderful beech-tree smell. Michael was there, today, standing near the swing-seat, his back to the cap-stoned well. Geraint Morris hesitated, glanced at his watch, wandered across the grass. Setting his heavy leather bag on the ground, he beckoned the young man. Both sat on the swing seat, moving gently in the morning breezes.

– Well, Michael? How's tricks?

Michael's mouth opened, gave out an enthusiastic humming. Dr Morris smiled, nodded vigorously. Over time they had grown to know and like each other pretty well. The sun came out of a deep cloud, emblazoning everything. And a new breeze wafted in, taking the doctor and his friend swinging in and out of that warm dazzle of summer.

– Going to be a scorcher, eh?

More watery sounds at the doctor's side. For an instant Dr Morris was reminded of an amiable spaniel, then with a pang of conscience he remembered that this creature was just as human as himself. Something gleamed in the boy's hand, he saw.

– What's that you've got there?

Michael held up the stone in two long, sculptured fingers, like some holy relic. It was a piece of crystal, dusty from the shoe-box in Michael's bedroom where it had lain for years. Geraint Morris read a curling label, printed in Indian ink.

*Crystals of Silica*

– Quartz?

Michael nodded eagerly.

– Where did you find it?

Michael's hand pointed eagerly up towards the woodlands beyond the house. The doctor studied the rock again. It looked old, worn down, very beautiful. Did it come from one of those iron-ore levels, he wondered to himself, carried out in a miner's pocket, maybe?

– Did you find it near one of those caves, mmm?

Michael's eyes met his. Opaque, far away from everyday logics. Dr Morris sighed, returned the stone. Maybe one day there would be a miracle and they would find a cure for this terrible disorder. Or at least something to take which didn't turn them into puppets on a string. A buzzard mewed sadly to its mate, far off, high above the sheep-grazing slopes of Penlan hill. Geraint Morris leant back, let the warmth of the morning sunshine and the quiet swing of the seat take away his train of thoughts. Around him now, the drowsy buzz of a bumble, the soft coo of a wood-pigeon.

– You know something, Michael? I'd give my left arm to have a house like this. Zina and I live down by the river. It's lovely in its way, but at times in the year like this we seem to get everything the factories up the valley pour out. You should smell the water some days! Then there's the railway and all those coal-wagons rattling past day and night. I tell you, sometimes we get no peace with them for a week!

The doctor paused, yawned expansively, drank in some more of that refreshing Ivy Cottage air.

– But here, you see, Michael. Close to the hill with all these beautiful trees around you. You can get to the heart of things. Make for yourself a real happiness –

Doctor Morris halted guiltily, recalling the reason for his visit. Glancing furtively to his right he contemplated Michael's calm, unfathomable features, sliding in and out of the sun. Well, let's hope he gets a better life of it now, after all this business. The doctor gave Michael's thick hair a cheerful tousle, rose to his feet.

– Better go in and see your mum and dad.

Michael hummed and warbled incomprehensibly. He looked on placidly, as Dr Morris picked up his leather bag, wandered around the side of the house towards the front-door. A wave of his hand into the dimness beyond the hallway window. Through unwashed glass, a face loomed, a hand waved back. Arthur finally appeared at the door. The two men shook hands warmly.

– How is she today, then, Arthur?

– Oh, you know – about the same.

Dr Morris studied the man's hollowed eyes. He must remember to suggest something for Arthur's sleep before he went. They entered the house, leaving all the sun behind.

– What are you reading these days, mmm? Finished with that Sigmund Freud? The fellow drove me half-mad at college, I can tell you! Alright, I'll admit there's a lot more to a Man than what he thinks he feels. But all that stuff about falling in love with your own mother –

A heavy brew of stale sweat and tobacco-smoke met the young doctor as they reached the kitchen, cutting off all further conversation. Ever professional, Dr Morris recovered himself, turned, beamed at his host.

– Now where is our patient?

She was not far away, as both knew. Two weeks before her bed had been brought downstairs to the little-used parlour by two burly village labourers. A day later a van had arrived from the hospital with a commode. Now the dying woman could spend a few short minutes each day, next to the window, drinking in a scent of roses and lupins and ivy-leaves. Violaceae's face was still lit by that same, bewildering softness. But there had been no further words on the subject between husband and wife.

– Doctor – is it you?

A feeble cry, drifting up to the two men as they stood there amidst the oppressive odours of the kitchen. The doctor strode forward.

– Ah – ha – I know that voice!

The parlour was dark and still. Another man might almost have missed that tiny form, beneath the thin sheets. But Dr Morris knew well how that illness took a person, shrinking them, inch by inch.

– Make the doctor some tea, dear.

Arthur nodded politely, hurriedly withdrew. Dr Morris set his bag at the foot of the bed, looked around for a straight chair. Violet raised a thin hand, like a constable stopping traffic.

– No. Not today. Sit here beside me, doctor. I want you to listen to something before Arthur gets back.

Geraint Morris was struck by the tranquillity of her voice, which seemed a world away from disease. He sat down on the bed, gazing into those watery blue eyes that suddenly seemed so young and girlish. She made a sign and so he obediently plumped the pillows behind her withered back.

– Better?

– Yes, thank you, doctor.

The chink of best Sunday-china in the kitchen. A pad of busy feet, assembling milk and sugar and Nice biscuits. Then the dying woman's voice again, in the gloom, sounding just as equable and sure.

– It's a funny thing. I thought it had all ended, you see, all those years ago, when Annie ran out across that road. It was the way the lorry left her, the way her little arms and legs all got – mixed up. But her face. Not a scratch, just think of that! I remember there was a bit of her hair that had got free of her ribbon and was waving about on the ground. I wanted to touch it so badly, because it seemed as if it was the very last bit of her that was alive. You see, doctor? You understand? You think to yourself after a thing like that, *nothing else can happen, there's no room for anything else.* And there isn't. Not after years and years. Except hate, of course. There was always room for that.

Violaceae ran out of breath, at last. She had probably spoken more words at one time than she had done in twenty years. Dr Morris gazed down at a printed rose-spray on the counterpane, bewildered.

– But, you see, doctor – the funny thing is – I know I love him now, despite everything.

The man braved those liquid, pain-filled eyes. Was she talking of her husband, or her son? He dared not ask.

– I used to watch him as he lit that stinking old pipe of his, or peered down through those stupid glasses at some book or other – and if there'd been a loaded shot-gun on the table I would have picked it up and used it. Can you understand that, doctor? Can you?

Doctor Morris made himself nod. She smiled sadly. A stab of cancer crossed her face, disappeared into some nebulous place within. Geraint Morris thought of that extra ampoule of morphine he had thoughtfully stowed in his satchel. No. Wait. Let her say it all. Who knows? It might be her last chance.

– As for Michael, I suppose I blamed him for being the one who lived on after Anne. But when he came home that night from Aldershot, all covered in his own filth – something broke. I sat in the kitchen and cried. Can you imagine that? Me! Crying real tears! I hadn't done that since I was a girl! But then they went away, of course. And so by the time he came home from hospital that day I hated him just as much as before. It hadn't gone, see. The tears hadn't got rid of it. Am I a bad woman, doctor? Tell me truly. Am I evil?

– Please – rest now – you must –

– No!

Her fingers gripped tight, taking his breath away. Words hissed close to his ear, full of fury.

– I have to! – Don't you understand! – I must!

Dr Morris nodded, in a dream. Somewhere in a world beyond, a kettle was hissing in the kitchen, feet creaked anxiously this way and that. Further off, another sound, fainter: a swing-seat, rocked endlessly back and forth. Was he imagining it? Violet's bony fingers were still there, real enough, digging into the soft flesh of his upper-arm. Dr Morris experienced an insane desire to leap out of the room, flee, never to return. Instead, he listened on, as he knew he must.

– The worst thing is when you wake up – at three or four in the morning – and you think to yourself, *It'll never be over, this business – not even when I'm dead!*

– Please – you really must –

– No! Wait! You have to wait! I want to ask you one thing, you see, before my husband comes back –

Fingers, digging ever deeper. Liquid eyes staring into the heart of who and what he was. Geraint Morris suddenly found himself remembering a day not so long ago when he clung to a muddy West-Welsh scarp in the driving rain. What could he do to save himself? Nothing. Just cling on. Hope some miracle would set him free.

– I want you to say it, you see, doctor – whatever you think inside– I want you to tell me!

Geraint Morris felt a tremor go through him. The room seemed dark as a pit. Just a woman's face, glimmering there, out of nothing. The young man swallowed hard, prepared –

But then Arthur was suddenly bustling in, balancing a tray, ludicrously over-laden, in his trembling fingers.

– I wonder, doctor – could you pull up that chair?

Geraint Morris rose hastily, took a step, halted, feeling Violet's fingers still tight upon him. The sound of her hissed whisper, inside him, like some childhood ghost.

– Well? Dr Morris? What d'you say?

Geraint Morris gazed deep. Time seemed to slow, like ripples disappearing in a woodland pool. Words, from some primordial place, crossing the void.

*Yes, Violet. You are forgiven*

The man heard himself in astonishment. A dizzy lightness raced through everything. The room came back, ungainly bed, dented chairs, shabby curtains. How easy it was, after all! Outside, a breeze down from the mountain sent beech-branches hissing everywhere. Dr Morris found himself grinning stupidly at a pair of confused-looking pebble-lenses.

– Well, Arthur? What are you gawping at!

Arthur bit anxiously on his pipe-stem, hurriedly set down the tray. The door creaked behind them. It was Michael's pale face, peering calmly in.

– There you are! Have we got enough cups?

Geraint Morris gratefully took his tea-cup, drank deep. Although the dying woman's fingers had gone away, the doctor noticed there was a white place still on his arm, where they had been.

A week later, Violaceae died peacefully in her sleep. All three women came down in the train from Penclydach to lay out their dead sister. Arthur could not bear the sound of their tearful voices and so he went out into the garden for a smoke. Michael had been taken on a day-trip to Cardiff Museum by a thoughtful neighbour. The fifty-five-year-old man found himself standing next to the lip of the covered well. It had rained briefly an hour or so earlier. In the wet grass near his foot, something gleamed. He picked it up. It was a piece of quartz from Michael's shoe-box, still with its label. How on earth had it got there? Arthur stuffed the fragment into his jacket-pocket, turned towards that black square of parlour-window, beyond which lay his wife, still as a photograph.

He had cried almost to sickness the day before. He would weep again, he knew, before the day was out. But now, just for this brief time, Arthur felt calm and clear. Suddenly a phrase appeared in his mind, huge, dramatic, like a banner draped across the blue of the sky.

*You have to carry on*

Four days later Arthur held his son's hand firmly as they watched a flower-strewn coffin sliding unsteadily out of sight, taking Violaceae from them for the very last time. The day before, Michael had started searching the house for his dead mother. The boy hurried busily from room to room, opening every cupboard he could find. No-one tried to stop him. What was the point? Now, today, it was as if the truth had somehow got down to those nebulous recesses of his mind.

– Alright, boy?

Michael nodded slowly. They turned together, wandered towards the cemetery gates.

That night, father and son sat in the kitchen eating bowls of Aunt Lilly's rice-pudding in silence. The sisters had left two hours before, making Arthur swear he would ring them tomorrow first thing, without fail. Now the house was very still. Arthur finally rose, lit his pipe with a spill from the fire. There, on the mantelpiece, his wife's pack of cards. Once, bright and gleaming inside Mr Champion's shop-display. Today, dulled, grimed with all those years of noisy village-hall whist. The man picked them up, fanned the pack curiously. An urgent moaning behind him. Arthur turned, smiled softly towards his son.

– You really think so?

More animated warblings.

– Righto.

The man sat opposite his son at the table, dealt hamfistedly. They began to play something that vaguely resembled rummy. Finally, as darkness came, Arthur stacked the cards and put them away in a cupboard forever. Father and son wandered out of the house, found themselves on the garden path, contemplating a cloud-covered night-sky.

– They bring you this little jar, see. We'll need to put her somewhere nice, mmm? Some people like their ashes to be thrown in the sea, but I don't think she had much feeling for that. What d'you think, boy? Where d'you think she'd finally want to be?

A week later a heavy parcel arrived in the house, bearing a smudged crematorium stamp. Arthur and Michael went out into the garden, armed with two spades from the shed. Finally they managed to lever back that slab of ancient, lichen-covered Penlan stone. They stood together, then, stared down into the well's inky depths.

– You really think so, Michael?

Michael waved his arms eagerly. And so Arthur took up the jar, handed it across. The boy opened the lid, stared down at a fine powder which did not look at all like his mother. His fingers made a shovel-shape, dipped curiously. Then he kneeled close to the lip of the well, sent a tentative shower into the black. Another. Another ... Arthur leant forward to see better. As the fragments flew briefly through the soft, late-afternoon air, the man thought he saw their greyness turned to a bright, lapis-lazuli blue.

Two hundred miles or so north of this sunny spot, on a stretch of slow-moving, scum-covered Mersey-river, Pamela Watson paused in her walk, mid-stride. The hem of the twelve-year-old's cheap print-frock had got caught in a bramble. The little girl bit her lip, knelt to unpick her dress. But then, as her measles-scarred arm strained forward to untrap one last bit of hem, she lost balance, tumbled down the embankment.
– Bloody hell!
Lying carelessly across mounds of filthy grass, Pamela examined a dribble of dark blood, oozing from the softness of her arm. Her pretty face, paled, puckered. A piece of broken beer-bottle must have got in the way as she fell. The pain of it hit her at last. She rose, sobbing, stumbling wildly home.
– Mam – mam – !
Many years later, the county pathologist who examined Pamela Watson's body noted this self-same wound, now a small scar only visible to the expert. The pretty young woman had been strangled by her own chiffon scarf in a piece of Penlan woodland less than a mile from where the remains of Violaceae now lay. Arthur and Michael were sitting as usual in Ivy Cottage's front-room on that damp night in early November, 1963, when Pamela's murder was said to have taken place. The tiniest fragment of a cry may perhaps have drifted up to them, across the valley. Deep in his latest volume of Jungian metaphysics, Arthur would have heard nothing. But a slight flicker under Michael's drugged left eye might have shown that he had.

# Stripped

*The Tenth Station. Jesus is Stripped of His Garments.*
*"My Most Innocent Lord,*
*By the Merits of the Torment Thou hast felt,*
*Help me to Strip myself of all Affection to Things of Earth . . ."*

Pamela Watson grew up in a small, nondescript town marooned between the slow-moving waters of the Mersey and the busy murkiness of the Manchester Ship Canal. In a world of smudged greys and ochres, the atmosphere made heavy by various admixtures from the soap and leather factories, her face preserved – at least for its first fifteen years – a surprising openness and innocence.

At secondary-modern school in the mid-fifties, she made numerous impatient doodles at the back of a class of forty or more scabby faces, avoiding the form-mistress's predatory eyes. Textbooks felt heavy and alien beneath her paint-cracked fingernails. Writing, when it came, seemed such a slow, pointless business. At break-time, she stood restlessly on the chalk-marked tarmac with a clutch of other fourth-formers, comparing stiletto-points and make-up plans, but even then she never felt easy inside herself. Only on the school's narrow cinder-track was everything suddenly and wonderfully different. Here she felt free, tearing around, circuit after circuit, arms and legs flailing. Once she came second at an Inter-school Hundred-yards Championship Final, and for a whole week the thrill of it lived within her. But her mother, weighed down by factory-shifts, fist-happy boyfriends and the never-never, didn't seem that interested. And so Pamela went off alone more and more to hover in the twilight outside local pubs and clubs, where she discovered that, with the right dimpled smile, men gave you that funny, hungry look which made you feel wanted at last.

One day she went with her best friend, Bee, to an expensive department-store in the middle of the town. There, in the privacy of the changing-room, each girl donned half-a-dozen cashmere jumpers, before striding out of the shop smiling simperingly at the assistants along the way. Giggling triumphantly, they raced down the High Street, blowing raspberries up at the grey, forbidding windows of the Municipal Hall.

– Naa – naa – naa-naa – naa – !

One summer's evening a thin, slick-backed nineteen-year-old offered Pam a ride on his shiny BSA 250 and they whizzed off, out of town, in search of The Blackpool Lights. All along West Street she buried her head in the warmth of the boy's fur-lined jacket-collar – and life seemed suddenly full of magical possibilities. They never found the lights, nor Blackpool for that matter, but when they got back to the town their faces met clumsily in the darkness of Tetford Locks and she felt his tongue inside her mouth, slippery as a fish. She ran blindly all the way home that night. In the bare-bulbed brightness of the Watson front-room, her mother gazed at her daughter's flushed face with weary bitterness.

– Who is he, then?

– Don't know what you mean –

– Don't lie to me, my girl!

Then, grabbing her hard, pulling her across the cigarette-scarred carpet, hissing hot wetness into her ear.

– Men ruin everything, you'll see.

Perhaps Pamela should have listened to her mother, that one time. A year later, in the long grass behind the swings of Coronation Park, Pamela let a thirty-two-year-old scaffolder from Liverpool come heavily into her and thought to herself when it was all over, and he was fumbling hurriedly with his flies in the dark – well, at least now I know what it's like.

Next morning, studying her reflection in a cracked bathroom mirror, she gave herself that special smile no-one else saw, and made her big decision. Life was never going to be different in this hole. If Pam Watson wanted to live, she had to get away.

And so in the spring of 1960, Pamela braved her mother's tears and curses – and moved to Birmingham. Dyeing her hair ash-blond, she began looking for work, threading her way through a bewildering, neon-lit city-centre. Her pretty features and soft brown eyes gave her one shop-assistant's job after another, but she never wanted to stay. After a few months, Bee came to share a tiny first-floor flat. Together, they roamed the night-time streets, armed with the latest pleated skirts and wide silver belts, in search of adventure. Pam soon learnt how to toy with her gin-and-orange on a high bar-stool, showing enough of her nylons to draw a good man with ready cash. At first it was just for the fun of free drinks and flirtation, but then one night a thirty-six-year-old accounts-manager took her to his parked Morris Minor and afterwards pushed a crisp ten-shilling note between her fingers.

– Don't be silly, Eddy!
– Why not? You deserve it!

After that, Bee went moody and silent. Some days she passed her best friend in the flat without so much as a glance. A month later, Pam returned from work to find a clumsily-written letter on the sofa.

*Some of us got pride*

Pam screwed up the note, chucked it in the grate. Let her go back home! Stupid ninny! A week later, Pamela Watson gave up the last of her shop-assistant's jobs, because she calculated that she was bringing in enough night-time cash now to live comfortably. A fortnight went by, and a good run of punters. At the end of the month she went into an electrical shop in the High Street and bought herself a walnut-finish TV, just like the one in the adverts.

Winter came. Pamela was doing pretty well, but something about this formless city with its grey, thin-lipped population, made her dissatisfied. One night, waiting outside the Moon and Sixpence, a man came up out of the shadows, stinking of whisky. She made to turn away, then saw the flick-knife, gleaming in his hand. A few minutes later, she let him do it the way he wanted, at the back of a railway-shed. He slunk off without a word. She was unharmed, thank the Lord, but next morning, painting on a new face in the mirror, she remembered the nice little Italian she'd met the other week from Cardiff who said he could set her up proper down there and only take a small cut. Tiger Bay sounded exotic, mysterious, much better than this dump!

– Well then, Pam? Why not?

And so Pamela Watson moved to Cardiff's docklands in the autumn of 1961, quickly warming to Butetown's lively, multi-racial community. Such a pleasant, happy-go-lucky thing! the neighbours later told reporters. Who could ever imagine anything nasty happening to a girl like that? But the truth was rather more complicated than those easy sentimentalities, offered up for public consumption in a local rag. The narrow, garrulous streets of the docks, constantly intersecting as in some enormous crossword-puzzle, excited Pamela – but also made her anxious, enervated. Working now both for herself and her voracious new employer, she needed more daily business to get by. Pam grew less careful with clients and with the law. Finally, after two cautions, she came before the local Magistrates on a charge of solicitation. It was a warm day in August. She grinned and waved towards her friends in the public gallery as she click-clicked out of the courtroom in her high-heels, with only a small fine. Two months later, her pimp came before a judge on a more serious charge. It was only then, at the end of the trial, that Pamela learnt that her employer had been to prison three times already. The little Italian laughed in their faces as he was told it was to be two whole years, this time. Pam smiled too, to show defiance. But outside on the street, the girl found herself suddenly in floods of tears.

Alone, Pamela aimlessly wandered the Butetown streets. Her soft brown eyes had become dulled. Her make-up, smudged, carelessly applied. One day she read a hand-written Post Office advertisement and went into a poky corner-shop next to the fruit-market, where she bought a grey, starved-looking kitten. She christened him Smoky. For weeks she fussed over the tiny creature at home, between jobs. Then one night the cat jumped out of a downstairs-window and never came back and suddenly Pamela Watson felt she was the loneliest person in all the world.

She went back home over that final Christmas of 1962. It was the last time she was ever to see her mother. They embraced in the narrow hallway amidst those familiar smells of house-damp and sour milk. The older woman felt her daughter's hot tears on her neck, and pulled hurriedly away.

– You must be hungry! Are you hungry?

They sat awkwardly in the kitchen. Pamela's mother had tried not to believe all that whispered gossip since Bee came home from Birmingham, yet now, glancing furtively at her daughter's mask-like features, she knew the worst. The shame of it filled her with a rage. Yet it was the festive season, hardly the moment to have a row. And so the poor woman said nothing that day, nor the next, and Pamela stayed on in the house long enough to eat a Christmas dinner of fried chicken, mash and processed peas. Two days later, on the doorstep, as her daughter made to leave, Pamela's mother suddenly felt a stab in her heart. Changing her mind, she thrust into her daughter's bewildered hands the Christmas present she had spent three weeks' rent-money to buy. Pam tore open the fancy-paper, stared down at a gleaming, stainless-steel Timex wristwatch.

– Mam, you shouldn't have!

But her mother was already turning away, returning into the house. It was then, at that moment when the door slammed shut, that Pamela understood.

*She knows everything*

Pamela Watson returned to Wales with quiet desolation lingering in those heavily-mascarared eyes. The flat in Llanelli Place smelt foul, full of shame. Spring came at last, with a pale, liquidish sun over the Bristol Channel. Pamela still knew how to exchange jokes with her neighbours and bring clients giggling home after the bars were shut, but when she was alone in her bedroom at last, the young woman's face grew empty, lifeless.

June, 1963. Just a few short months before the end. Pam had gone a hundred miles north to the prison to tell Luciano she did not want him back. His small-featured face looked child-like. But the howl he made was adult enough, echoing through the prison. Returning home on a slow-stopping train, the young woman thought back to that girl, tearing along a cinder-track, arms flailing. Was there any way back? Pamela stared out of the carriage-window, saw how the sun trailed endless patterns of gold and lemon through a succession of sprawling Welsh woodlands. If only she had a nice house in the country, with trees all around!

Suddenly, as in a vision, Pamela Watson saw herself and a young man wandering through a dappled beech-glade, picking bluebells. A heady scent of blossom filled the carriage. She opened her eyes with an ache of sadness, noticed on the other side of the compartment a middle-aged man, reading a slim volume of poetry with the assistance of a pair of old-fashioned spectacles. The man looked up, peered at her, his eyes curiously enlarged. Pam smiled, without quite knowing why. The man smiled back.

Half-an-hour later the train arrived at Cardiff Queen Street. As Pamela emerged onto a crowded platform she glimpsed her fellow-passenger meeting a younger man, evidently his son. For a moment, the boy's eyes met hers through a blur of bodies. They were wide, unfocused, vividly blue. Pam found herself looking hurriedly away. What had so disturbed her? She saw now how his large hands made constant feather-like movements at his side. Poor dab! Probably some mental defective, like that Sam in standard-three, who could never keep his face still. Pamela turned, strode off towards Bute Street and the Docks.

Four months later, on that fateful day at the end of October, 1963, Pamela Watson ate a perfunctory supper of fish-cakes and chips straight out of the newspaper-wrapping. Outside, it was raining again. There had been sharp autumn showers all day. The radio said they were happening all over Wales. At about seven in the evening a late sun finally appeared over Cardiff's slate-roofed skyline, as the young woman stepped out of her Tiger Bay flat, dressed for work in a sky-blue jumper, short navy skirt, gold belt, and fish-net stockings. Knotted around her neck was her favourite black chiffon scarf.

During the next hour or so, Pamela was observed by various local people across the Butetown streets, assiduously *plying her trade*. One later deposed to police that he had seen *a young woman in blue* talking with a *stocky gentleman*, in the driving-seat of his green Morris van. Another reported *a man of Jewish appearance* conversing with the *lady in question* at about eight o' clock next to the Customs House. After that – nothing. Pamela Watson was never seen alive again.

Two days later, on a sunny Sunday morning, four young schoolboys arrived at Penlan woods, all the way from Glynmaes village in search of fossils. They made their way eagerly to a small cave-entrance they had been told of, hidden high up on Penlan's birch-clad slopes. At half-past eleven they found the place. The dark gap in the smooth, weather-worn limestone was just wide enough to let them in, one by one, eyes bright with anticipation. Inside, hunching their shoulders against the dampness of the rock, the boys felt that icy breath from the deep. Hurriedly switching on a motley collection of bicycle lamps and cracking jokes to keep up their spirits – they ventured forward.

It was Sidney Whitcombe who first saw her, half-an-hour later, draped across a narrow ledge, beneath two-hundred and fifty feet of iron-ore ventilator-shaft. A few moments earlier, Danny Perkins had excitedly picked up a Timex stainless-steel wristwatch he had seen on the cave-floor, gleaming under his torch-beam. This was all but forgotten, now, however, as, mute with terror, the four youngsters trained trembling lights on the body. Jumper, torn, stained. Skirt, bunched up high to the waist. Scarf knotted deep in the neck. Soft brown eyes, gazing piteously out at eternity.

The boys dropped everything, fled screaming from the spot.

Old Mr Champion had to summon up his best human skills later that morning, when the teenagers arrived panting and hysterical inside his corner-shop. After calming them down as best he could, they proceeded in a straggling procession to the nearest public-telephone, some fifty yards down the road. The police duly arrived. There was a confused conference on the pavement. Someone thought of Dr Morris. A young constable was dispatched to find him. Luckily he was at home, reading the London pages of the newspaper. When mention was made of the iron-ore cave, the middle-aged doctor's eyes lit up oddly.

– Won't be a minute. I'll just get my bag.

By lunch-time, the police search-party had reached the cave entrance, augmented by members of a local RAF Rescue Team equipped with arc-lights, who happened to be training close by. Little Sidney Whitcombe led the way, whimpering to himself as they left the comfort of daylight behind. Splashing through weirdly-lit tunnels, full of predatory shapes, Sidney experienced his second panic-attack of the day. Geraint Morris had to sit him down on a rock for a few minutes of gentle reassurance, before they were able to continue. Finally, after over an hour of awkward stumbling, they reached the ledge where the boys said the woman lay. For a brief moment, Dr Morris recalled the time, years before, when he had excitedly planned a pot-holing trip to this very place. It had never quite happened, what with the children and the practice and everything. But was that the glimmering of an underground lake over there?

What was it called? Ah, yes. Blue Waters!

A constable shone his torch in a different direction and pointed. They all grew quiet, contemplating Pamela Watson's sad, mascara-smeared eyes. Sidney was led to one side. Arc lights were carefully set up and positioned. The police and RAF investigators began their grim work. It was around four in the afternoon by the time their job was complete, and all the photographs taken. The corpse was gently lifted onto a stretcher to begin its journey back. By now young Sidney's eyes had a dull, dilated look to them and he made no sound at all as Pamela Watson's body, trailing a single lock of dyed-blond hair, passed him by. All the way back through the caverns, the boy kept muttering about a lost wristwatch, but no-one took any notice.

Truth to tell, all, including the doctor, were hungering now for that tiny fissure of light which meant order and sanity and home. It finally came and in due course they were back on the surface. Dark rain-clouds had formed whilst they had been away, and now loud drops were pattering about them on the soft, leaf-covered woodland floor. Half a mile away, high up on Penlan hill, stood a clutch of busy figures and the shape of a rope-cordon around the ventilator-shaft entrance where the poor woman had been thrown down. Geraint Morris put Sidney in the care of a local nurse, wandered up the hill to see.

It was not a very picturesque spot next to the shaft, with brambles and nettles spewing everywhere. As the doctor arrived at the cordon, forensic experts were advancing slowly through the bushes with sticks, bent low. Not far away, was a rutted farm-track, where more police were crouched, hurriedly taking plaster-casts in the mud before the rain obliterated everything. Geraint Morris smiled grimly. This was a well-known spot for lovers. As if confirming the fact, he noticed right next to his shoe the shape of a used Frenchie, glimmering primrose-like in the gloom.

– There won't be many more of them here, after today!

An excited shout. Two constables raced past him, ducking under the ropes. They had found something. Dr Morris stepped forward to see. There, inside a plastic bag, one of Pamela Watson's missing stilettos. Before dark they found the other, along with the young woman's Italian-style clasp-handbag. In the days that followed there was talk of a missing wristwatch, but no-one remembered little Sidney Whitcombe's ramblings as the search-party trekked out of the caves. As for poor Sidney himself, he was now in Anglesey with a kindly aunt and uncle who fed him chips every day for comfort.

Geraint Morris was overcome with exhaustion when he got home that night. Zina had heard the news already from a noisy lane of neighbours. Seeing her husband's haggard features, she said nothing, hurriedly leaving the room to make up a supper-tray.

The children were finally all in bed. The man ate his ham sandwiches in silence in the parlour. Zina quietly darned socks opposite. Her husband looked up at her suddenly.

– I saw the Blue Water.

She stared, confused.

– Remember? The lake I told you about, under Penlan hill.

– Oh – yes –

They looked at each other in the half-light. Somewhere not far away was a dream-like sound of ripples from the river. Both were thinking of that other water, next to the dead woman under the earth.

– They say she was a prostitute. But her face. It looked so – so innocent somehow –

– Shouldn't it be?

Her eyes were upon him, gently challenging. He nodded sadly. She was right, of course. Yet it still seemed so strange, he considered, after all the poor girl must have gone through down there in Tiger Bay. God knows, you don't have to be a doctor to see how lives get scarred by their circumstances. Not just on the surface, but deep down, too. Zina's voice broke into his musing at last.

– I wonder who did it.

He said nothing. Silence, then the whimper of their youngest child upstairs. Zina hurriedly got up, disappeared. Geraint Morris was alone in the room, sipping the last of his tea. Just river-ripples, then the wind rose outside and from across the valley came the creak of a thousand shifting beech-branches. The doctor suddenly thought of them, those two solitary men in that beautiful tree-ringed house. They were only half a mile away from where she died. Had they heard Pamela Watson's last screams?

# Nailed

> The Eleventh Station. Jesus is Nailed to the Cross.
> *"My Lord, loaded with Contempt*
> *Nail my Heart to Thy Feet*
> *That it may ever more remain there . . ."*

A few days later the local newspapers announced that a Scotland Yard man, Chief Superintendent Thomas Mildmay, was now in charge of the case, heading up a team of twenty-five detectives.

*No stone will be left unturned*

Why did they always say that? Geraint Morris turned to the inside pages of his breakfast newspaper although the surgery was already filling up, he knew. On page five, a photograph of the deceased. The doctor stared at it in confusion, until he realised that it must have been taken at school, years before Pamela had dyed her dark hair blonde to improve her business.

– I wonder what drove her to it.

Zina took the newspaper from him, pursing her lips. Dr Morris wandered to the living-room window, gazed out.

– No mention of a father. Did you notice that, Zina? And she was born during the war.

– Out of wedlock?

– It's possible, isn't it? And it might account somehow for what the poor girl did with her life.

They exchanged glances, looked away. It was probably best not to pursue such questions. After all, what did that matter now? Zina folded the newspaper, rose, stood beside him at the window. Far off was the shape of the mountain. From here it looked like the head of a mythical beast.

– To end your life like that – plunging down –
– Already dead, Zina. Remember the chiffon scarf. She knew nothing.
– Of course. It's just that – well – even then –
– Yes, I know.

Geraint Morris opened a silver cigarette-case, lit a Players Number-Three. Zina stared at her husband in surprise. He smoked just three or four in a whole week – and never in the morning.

– They want to see me.
– Those Scotland Yard people?
– Just loose ends they said. I'll pop over, after surgery.

It turned out that Tom Mildmay was a football fan like himself. They exchanged statistics on cup finals, between forensic discussion.

– 1927. Cardiff One, Arsenal Nil. The only time the Cup went out of England!

It made the business more human. But that night the doctor still dreamt of Pamela Watson. She was as she looked in that newspaper photograph, lying next to the weir, blood mingling with her black tresses. He woke, drugged. Who was that ungainly man, sitting next to her, holding her hand?

– Of course. Michael. Poor lad. Why on earth did I think of him?

A week passed. Anxious for progress, the police began a sweep of mass-interviews throughout the Docks. There were some early leads, chewed over eagerly in the local press – but they came to nothing. Then, on a dull, drizzly Thursday morning, Pamela Watson's funeral took place at Pantmawr, just a few miles from where her life had violently ended. The night before, her mother had arrived from Cheshire, with enough money borrowed from neighbours for a cheap city-centre hotel. Gripping the hem of her threadbare overcoat, the woman stared blankly down at that oblong of bright fresh earth where her daughter now lay.

– She'd never talk, d'you see? If she'd have talked –

Her words faltered. No-one was listening. Just a few damp faces across the grass, friends and neighbours from Butetown, who didn't know this plain-faced woman from Adam. They finally wandered off, making for the local pub. Carol Watson was left alone, twisting a grubby handkerchief over and over.

– If she'd have said – then maybe –

A cold north wind swept down from the Valleys and hit her cheeks with a fusillade of tiny droplets. She shivered, shrugged, turned away from her daughter for the last time. As she walked quickly away across the graveyard, a small blackbird alighted on the new, glistening earth, looking for food.

There were two theories early on about the murder. The first, favoured by local police, was that Pam Watson had been killed somewhere in Tiger Bay, probably by one of her clients, then taken seven miles north in the back of the man's car to Penlan wood. The murderer, a Cardiff man, may well have known about that ventilator-shaft. It was not so far from the road, after all, and a popular spot with lovers. What better way to hide the terrible evidence of his crime? Somehow he had dragged the body through the bushes and over the edge, all under cover of darkness. But it was his peculiar ill-luck that the corpse hit that ledge, two hundred and fifty feet below – and an even more cruel twist of fate that to this dark spot, a mere two days later, came four young boys in search of fossils.

A second and more melodramatic theory, adopted by one or two Scotland Yard men, along with certain members of the press – suggested that Pamela was still alive when she arrived that night in Penlan wood. Driven there by one of her regulars, maybe – or, even more tantalisingly, by some mysterious boyfriend. There, in the darkness of the trees, the two had made love clumsily in the backseat. Was this all part of some perverse plan on the part of the man? Or did something go wrong in the car, releasing a terrible, unstoppable rage? Perhaps the poor girl had mocked at something he did – or failed to do! Who likes to be humiliated in such matters? Least of all, men of violence.

Then (these theorists continued with dark relish) his fingers must have suddenly tightened around the poor girl, making a grab for that chiffon scarf which was still knotted around her neck. Pamela Watson's wide, doe-like eyes must have stared, dazed, bewildered as he went on with his business. Her mouth at first tried to scream, then just gasped for breath. Her skin finally going cold and blue under the light of an autumn moon . . . She was dead. The man gazed about him, in panic. A sudden inspiration, then, as he remembered a pot-hole he had glimpsed a few months back, during a summer's jaunt. Wasn't it somewhere nearby? A few hectic minutes, sweating profusely as he dragged the body through the brambles (the police found a winding path of broken leaves and stems leading from the lane to the shaft), before he sent his lover down into the blackness with an exhilarated gasp of relief. Then, turning, staggering back to the car, crashing gears with wild abandon as he lurched his vehicle three-hundred-and-sixty degrees (plaster casts revealed at least four reversings performed recently in the muddy lane) to make his escape.

There was also a third theory, not held by many at first, but taken up later when more and more of Pamela Watson's clients produced watertight alibis.

The murderer wasn't from Cardiff at all. He was a local village boy.

Two weeks after the body's discovery, in the middle of November, scores of extra constables were drafted into the surrounding Penlan villages to commence house-to-house enquiries. By now the newspapers were filled with another much more dramatic murder, a crime which had taken place thousands of miles away, in broad daylight, on a crowded street in Dallas.

Arthur pored over these new lurid headlines, like the rest of the world, in a mood of anger and despair. Nearing retirement, the man found himself living now a more-or-less house-bound existence, with most of the day taken up caring for his thirty-three-year-old schizophrenic son. Two years ago, abruptly, he had stopped sending letters to London. There had been three court cases in all, over twelve long years: a Tribunal hearing, followed by two judicial appeals. All were lost, on the basis of written statements forwarded to the court by the Ministry of War. Despite numerous protests and petitions, Arthur's solicitor was never allowed to call military personnel to face cross-questioning in court. It was the law of the land.

– It's the army. What did you expect?

Michael's condition had stabilised somewhat over the years, so that now, in the autumn of 1963, he needed just a few of Professor Gilbert's tranquillisers, mainly to help him sleep at night. The boy's latest fad was for jig-saw puzzles. The ones he liked best, Arthur found, had pictures of aeroplanes on the cover. Today, on that Sunday in the mid-November, father and son were sitting diligently over the kitchen table. A score or more jig-saw pieces had found their home. Several hundred more lay scattered over the curling oilcloth. A dozen lay at the man-child's feet. Neither attempted to pick them up.

The constables' boots made strange crackling sounds on the paving-stones outside, as they approached. Arthur and Michael looked up in surprise. Two helmets were bobbing past the kitchen window. A peremptory rap on the back-door. Arthur rose hurriedly. He put a soft hand on his son's shoulder, as he passed.

– Nothing to worry about, mmm?

Michael's eyes gazed up at his father, wide, soft, ever-trusting.

There were two of them, both in their twenties, one carrying a grubby-looking roneoed questionnaire. The men arrived in the kitchen, helmets under their arms, nostrils wrinkling against the stale odours of the house.

– Won't take a moment.

– Cup of tea?

They shook their heads hurriedly. Arthur cleared various jig-saw pieces away, several dropping onto the floor. The men sat, looked curiously about them, produced pencils and notebooks.

– Just a few minutes of your time!

They smiled encouragingly. There was a pause. Michael's fingers began a little dance on top of the oilcloth. Arthur took them up with maternal care, patted them firmly on the young man's knee.

– You've heard about the case, I take it?

Arthur removed his spectacles, polishing them busily on a loose corner of his shirt.

– Poor thing. Hardly out of school! Why do people do such things?

Twenty minutes later the two constables emerged from the house, blinking against the light. They looked at each other meaningfully as they wandered down the garden path. Then, through the gate and out into the lane, they were suddenly chattering excitedly.

– See his face?
– That look in his eyes!
– Some sort of psychotic –
– Ring the hospital – find his notes!
– What drugs he's on and –
– Well, Jim? D'you think he might?
– All you need is a fit.
– Let's get on the blower to Wilf!

They raced along then, through dazzles of autumn sun.

Back in the cottage, Arthur leant over the washing-up bowl, his hands covered in bubbles, shaking violently.

– What is it, dad?
– Nothing son, get on with that game.

Michael resumed the jig-saw with obedient fingers. Moments passed. Somewhere, a car revved, ground into gear, drove off at speed. Arthur seemed far away, staring out at nothing.

– Lost one – where is it? – need help, dad –
– In a minute, lad.
– Come now please –
– I said later!

The wild shriek was out before he could stop it. Arthur turned contritely. His son bent his head, whimpering onto the oilcloth like a four-year-old. Arthur sat down beside him, took his hand in his.

– Sorry, boy – just a bit tired, see?

The boy's blue eyes were open, wide, questioning.

– Why did they ask all those things?

Arthur looked across at his son. In the twilight of the room, Michael's face was haloed by a shaft of golden, late-afternoon sun. Suddenly the older man found himself thinking of a crown of thorns. Of course. Even the right age for it! A wild laughter went through him, but he managed somehow to stifle it. Michael must have seen something, though, for he rose, stumbled across the room, bolted out of the house.

– Michael – ! Michael wait!

Racing footsteps, fading to nothing. Arthur was too tired and empty even to rise from his chair.

– Well, let him go.

Darkness fell. The garden was a mixture of dark blobs, now, with lines of paleness where the paths crossed. Arthur grew fearful, wandered this way and that, shouting out at the trees, but there was still no reply. At half-past eight he went back into the house, re-emerging moments later with his hat and stick. Michael hadn't been into the woods for years. A cold foreboding took hold of the man as he left the cottage behind him and found himself wandering through a maze of dark trees.

Michael! Michael!

Half a mile from the house, Arthur paused for breath. In front of him, the path divided in two. One way, up to the mountain-top; the other, across the valley to the birchwoods and the stream. Where now? Maybe he should just go back, phone the police –

– No! Not them!

Six hundred yards from the spot where Arthur stood, Michael had found the stream. This was the place where, aeons ago, he and his father had raced twigs through miniature rapids on a sunny summer's afternoon. Even tonight – after all the insulin and sodium amytal and electric shocks which came after – Michael smelt that piercing odour of wild peppermint which came all the way from his childhood.

The young man crossed the stream in one stride. He found himself in a grove of slender birch-trunks, straight as a regiment at parade. Michael's feet walked with steady purpose, now, as if they knew. Before him, quite suddenly, that pale, strangely rounded limestone – and the narrow gap of thicker darkness which was the cave-entrance he had not visited in a decade.

Michael knew what he had to do. Obstinately, he shoved himself through the crevice, inch by inch into the hillside. Finally, impossibly, his body was right inside. Michael stepped forward, feeling the cold fingers of the cavern clutching at every part of him. He journeyed deeper. The rustle of dry leaves and twigs which had been with him at first, gradually died away. Now, just his panting, and an odd, echoey cough. Finally he paused, caught breath. He must be quite deep, now. He cocked an ear, listened. For some moments, just a faint trickling of invisible water-courses, all around. Then suddenly, something faint but quite different. Michael strained his ears. Yes. No doubt about it. Whispering. Far off, but always coming nearer. Moments passed. Closer. Closer . . . Then, suddenly, the voice seemed right next to him. Words, eager, lively, all too familiar:

– Is that you, Mikey?

– Yes.

– Knew you'd come back in the end.

Michael peered into the black and finally saw a face, glimmering eerily like a Hollywood-star in a crowded picture-house. But how different Annie looked! No longer that impish five-year-old. Instead, her face was older, painted over with lurid make-up, and covered with a mass of dyed, ash-blond curls. With a lurch at his heart, he knew the truth.

– Of course. It was you all along.

As if in confirmation, a delicate sound now met Michael's ears for the very first time. Trembling, he crouched low in the cavern, fingering the rocky crevices at his feet. Finally his long fingers found what they were looking for. He rose up once more, stared down at a small object, glowing there in his fingers, and emitting, still, that faint, metallic sound.

It was a stainless-steel Timex.

– Yours, now, Mikey.

Michael tried to scream, but nothing came out – and his sister's face was already gone. Just that last friendly whisper, echoing to nothing. Michael stared, turned, stumbled headlong back the way he had come.

# Dying

> *The Twelfth Station. Our Lord Dies on the Cross.*
> *"Oh, my dying Jesus, I kiss Devoutly the Cross on which*
> *Thou didst Die for Love of me . . ."*

The police began their surveillance of Ivy Cottage as Christmas was approaching, in December 1963.

Arthur first noticed them, lingering inelegantly amongst the beech trunks, one wintry morning, when he came out early to collect the milk before it froze. Arthur heard an odd cough in the stillness, paused, peered through misty lenses – but they had already shuffled out of view. Had he imagined those dark blue helmet-tops just above the hedge? The old man turned, wandered inside, set a greasy kettle upon the stove. Outside a motor-bike suddenly started up, careering away noisily, just as the car had done on the day they came with the questionnaire. Arthur's heart quickened with fear.

Ever since the night when Michael had disappeared into Penlan wood, Arthur's soul had been troubled. The boy had finally returned to the house in the early hours, his face flushed, distracted, leaving oozing mud-stains on each of Ivy Cottage's fourteen stairs as he stumbled up to his bed. Later Arthur had crept up to his son's door, hesitated, politely knocked.

– Boy? Are you alright, boy?

Nothing. Not even a murmur or a tuneless hum. The man hesitated, wandered back to his own bedroom, where he stared at a tired reflection in the wardrobe mirror.

– At least he's back, eh? That's the main thing.

In his room, meanwhile, Michael sat hugging himself on the

narrow bed. Gripped in his left hand was that stainless-steel wristwatch, still chattering away insanely.

– An-nie – An-nie – An-nie – An-nie –

Michael stared at the illuminated hands and suddenly it was as if they were pointing up at him, like a pair of guardhouse squaddies. He hurled the terrible vision away, but still it gleamed mockingly at him from across the floor, lit now by the cold light of the moon. Michael felt his whole body shudder as it had done on a sweaty parade-ground years before.

– What did you say, laddie – mmm?

– I – I don't know, sergeant –

– Yes you do! You pile of steaming ugly shite!

Finally sleep took Michael in its embrace and he forgot about Aldershot and the wristwatch and poor Annie lying in that cold, wet Penlan cave. But when he woke next morning it was as if that endless, sing-song voice was shrieking through the whole house.

– An-nie – An-nie – An-nie – An-nie –

That was when the young man stumbled across the room and stamped at the tiny gleaming thing on the floor with his shoe until it was in a thousand pieces.

The voice was gone.

But it was then, when silence finally returned to the house, that Michael knew for certain. It was him. Of course! How could it be otherwise? He had done the thing the whole village was talking about. He had pushed the poor girl down into that terrible shaft.

How easy it felt suddenly! Michael cocked his ear and listened to the quiet of the morning. A robin was calling to its mate amongst the bare branches on the edge of the wood. Further off, the quick, excited bark of a sheepdog. Then, just the breathing of a gentle west wind. The moment was tranquil, uplifting even, for the young man, for he saw now that nothing had really changed since the day he had let his sister cross the tarmac to her death. Goodheart and Bailey were right. He was getting what he had always deserved.

Michael opened his eyes, smiled. A loaf-shape of soft morning sunshine climbed the wall next to his bed. He was so happy. There was nothing more to struggle against.

Father and son ate a silent lunch in the kitchen. Arthur knew something had changed. Watching his son stir that dollop of raspberry jam round and round on his plate, Arthur felt a sudden pang. How he had tried to love and protect his dear Christmas-born son over all the years! And for this! The utter powerlessness he felt now, gazing into the drugged opacity of his man-child's eyes! Arthur's whole body stiffened with fury. But he knew there was nothing he could do or say.

Over the next week, life preserved an appearance of normality. Through the day they walked silently past each other, like characters in a play. One night, Arthur woke with a jolt, sensing something. It was his son, standing by the bedroom door, staring down at his hands with a look of terror.

– What is it, boy?
– Nothing.
– Please – please tell me –

Utter sadness suddenly in his son's eyes. Arthur rose, clung to Michael.

– I'm scared, dad – I'm so scared –
– It's alright, son – I'm here with you. Always!

Then, guiding his thirty-three-year-old son back across the landing to his bedroom, tucking him underneath his blankets as if he were a six and blubbering into his sheets.

– Don't let them come – Please don't!

Arthur knew the next words, even before they came.

– Don't let them take me back to the guardhouse!

Gripping Michael's arm, at that, with furious conviction.

– I'll never let that happen, Michael. I give you my word.

An hour later Arthur still sat on the foot of the bed, watching his son falling into a deep sleep, helped by a hefty dose of Largactil. A question had formed itself deep down, although he did not quite have the means to put it into words.

*Could he have done it? Could he?*

Though he never once articulated it to himself, the insane doubt kept closing on him like some tiny, burrowing insect. And when, a few days later, he saw their bright blue uniforms lurking in the pale wintry woodland, a mere fifty yards from the house – Arthur's mind went numb with terror. How long had they been there spying? Why? What did they want? A terrible conviction took hold of the old man.

*They've been to the hospital*
*They know everything*

Michael did not seem to notice the police that day. He just wandered about the house, as usual, humming inconsequentially. Arthur noticed however that one of his hands was clenched shut, as if he was holding something for dear life.

– What you got there, lad?

Michael shook his head and smiled so appealingly that his father did not pursue the subject. Finally Arthur left the room, to peel potatoes for dinner. Alone, the young man opened his palm, saw with quiet satisfaction how the tiny watch-cog, chosen carefully from the bedroom floor, had ground into the softness of his flesh, producing a nice lot of blood.

It was close to Christmas. Arthur's humming child was about to be thirty-four years old. One morning Arthur made a decision. Leaving a bland note on the mantelpiece, he strode out of the house and climbed high into Penlan woods. He did not quite know which direction to take, but instinct took him all the same. Spiky branches formed complicated patterns against the whiteness of the winter sky. Occasionally there would the cough of a sheep, or the harsh, echoey cry of a magpie. Not much else to break the peace of this frozen December landscape. Finally the old man got to the spot. The rope-cordons had long gone, but there was enough mess and scuffing of the ground to mark out the place where the police had been.

Arthur stopped short, suddenly confused. There, right in front of him, a wall of bright, newly-cemented breeze-blocks. It was a strange sight in the middle of the trees, but Arthur quickly realised what it meant. After all it was perfectly sensible, when you came to think about it, for the authorities to block off the cave-entrance, once all the collecting of evidence was over.

*Once bitten, twice shy*

The man took a step closer, ran his fingers over that strange place where smooth cement-work met the bulbous shapes of weather-worn limestone. Funny to think of all that darkness, locked away, beyond – and even a lake, so they said –

It was at that moment, musing idly to himself, that Arthur noticed a mass of footprints all around him in the mud. A confused sense of familiarity took hold and then his body went colder than the day. Yes. It was Michael's shoes that had made them, scores, hundreds of restless steps. How many times had the boy been here since the cordons had gone? A terrible knowledge came upon him.

– Every night – since that first time – dear God!

Particles of fine dry snow began to fall from the sky above. Arthur stood watching them as they began to settle everywhere on branches, on dead leaves, even on the shiny dubbin of his shoe. It was as if everything was disappearing, inch by inch, to a white nothing.

Arthur swayed, turned, stumbled madly away.

Christmas morning came with a pretty sheen of winter sunshine over a speckled scatter of that same fine-particled snow. Arthur woke, gazed blankly at the old damp patch on his ceiling. Somewhere far off, *All through the Night* was playing on a village radio. For a brief moment the man seemed to see the face of his wife, there, on the pillow beside him, softened by the proximity of death. Tears rose in his eyes.

Our Saviour's Day. And Michael's too!

Then Arthur remembered the men outside, that ring of patient, starched-blue uniforms, waiting for their victim to break. The man rose from bed, pulled on his clothes. Had he fought with the authorities in London all these years to give way now to a bunch of local idiots? Let them make their accusations! His boy was innocent, just like that Other One, two thousand years before!

– If it's a fight they bloody want!

Arthur was fussing busily over breakfast things when a slow shuffle of slippered feet down Ivy Cottage's narrow stairs announced the arrival of his son. Michael sat obediently at the kitchen table. Before him, a huge, brightly-decorated parcel, prepared meticulously the night before.

– Go on, then. Open it!

Those long fingers, delving through layers of festive paper. Finally, reaching the grey-green cardboard covers of a dozen or more gramophone records, each with its neat printed label.

– All his symphonies. Every last one –

Michael took the top one out of its cover. The young man held it up high, squinting close. A myriad pattern of acetate grooves, there, caught by snow-filled light from the kitchen window. Funny to think of all that beautiful Beethoven hidden inside.

A dead beech-branch snapped, hardly twenty feet away. The record crashed to the floor in a thousand pieces. Arthur rose, lurched to the window. Constable Turpin stood there near the back-gate, his uniform flecked with snow. A ball of anger rose up to Arthur's throat. He strode across the room, flung open the door, hurled a wild shriek out at the trees.

– Do you know what day it is? Do you? Go! Get on out of it! Leave my poor Michael alone!

A lop-sided grin appeared momentarily on Turpin's face before he turned tail, crunching noisily away across the frost-covered woodland floor. Hot breath suddenly on Arthur's neck. The man looked around. Michael was there beside him, the whites of his eyes showing.

– Come along, lad. Inside, now. It's all over, mmm?

Luckily it was the first and least important symphony which was destroyed by Constable Turpin's clumsy footfall. And so the two of them had spent a pleasant Christmas night, playing the rest of the gramophone records, with Michael's arms flying joyfully about the room, just as they had done in those far off, innocent days of youth. Finally it was time for bed. Arthur rose, made wearily to the door. He found his son's arms suddenly tight around him.

– What is it Michael?

A flood of tears, now, dribbling inside his shirt-collar.

– Love – love you all –

– I know you do, boy. You don't have to say it.

The hallway clock chimed midnight. They climbed the fourteen stairs together, that night, hand in hand. Reaching the top, Michael made his father stop, listen. There, on the edge of senses, a child was singing.

*No crib for a bed*

Arthur thought of Geraint and Zina Morris, down in their cottage by the river. Was it their little eight-year-old maybe? People weren't all bad. Some were like saints. Even Mr Price-Richards and Mr Shinwell did what they could. It was those others, the people you never saw, people with no names, people who never came to court to testify. They were the worst. It was then, glancing down at his son's upturned palm that he noticed a fresh scar not unlike those made long ago by rusty Aldershot mess-tin lids. But his boy was already gone, wandering towards his room. Arthur sighed to himself to think what a tired imagination can do in the dark.

I'll be seeing ghosts, next!

A face, turning palely towards him in the yellow gloom.

– Goodnight, dad.

– Goodnight, Michael.

The bedroom door closed. Things will get better, Arthur thought to himself, as he wandered back across the landing. He grinned to himself, thinking of that stupid policeman racing off into the trees. He'd given him what's what! They wouldn't be coming back again in a hurry!

But they did. They were there the next morning, and the next, and the next.

Three months later, it happened. Looking back with the benefit of hindsight, Geraint Morris was surprised it took so long. It was a Sunday morning in early April, he remembered. The doctor and his wife were out in the garden, tasting a bit of real Spring sun for the first time, when the phone-call came, tinkling faintly from inside the house. Geraint hurried off to answer. He was gone for over ten minutes. When he came back out onto the lawn his face was as white as a sheet. Zina rose, gripped his arm.

– What's happened?

– Michael. Took the lot – that whole bottle I left –

The tragedy, it emerged, had taken place two hours before. In his hysteria poor Arthur had not known how to call the ambulance. Instead he had phoned the family miles away in Penclydach, sending everyone into a blind panic. In the end an ambulance somehow found the place. Too late. Michael was already slumped dying across the linoleum of the kitchen floor. They found an empty bottle of pills upstairs in the bathroom. Just a few were left, a pale trail of them twisting down the stairs. Arthur said later he watched his son come down those fourteen steps, very slow, as if he was in a dream.

– What was he thinking, then? Mmm What?

A stretcher was brought and the ambulance finally set off for the nearest hospital. All the way, Arthur sat holding his son's hand. It was odd to hear the alarm-bell jangling and see Michael's face so calm and peaceful. Arthur saw his whole life, then, laid out like a geometric line across the ether, with a small boy at the other end, lying on coal-stained Penclydach grass amongst a shoal of writhing sticklebacks.

– I should never have got up.

The ambulance lurched into the hospital grounds and Arthur's thoughts were sent off in a scatter as a crowd of doctors and nurses converged on the scene. His son was rushed off into Emergency. Some time later, perhaps twenty minutes or so, the old man came to himself, sitting in a bleak, white-painted waiting-room. Above him, a notice warned in stark capitals:

## HAVE YOU HAD YOUR BCG?

Bridget arrived on the scene from nowhere, carrying cups of tea bought from a nearby trolley. Arthur took his gratefully, but such was the trembling of his fingers that most got spilt on the floor. After a while the old man said he wanted a smoke and so Bridget went outside with him. They sat together on a bench next to some horse-chestnut trees, bare, spectral still in the gentle April sunshine. His sister-in-law tried to make conversation to take the poor man's mind away.

– Did you hear Bertrand Russell last week on the Home Service?

Arthur smiled, nodded, began to cry noisily, so they went back inside. He sat down again, just where he had before, next to the BCG sign. Dr Morris finally appeared from Intensive Care where he had been in conference with the experts for half-an-hour. His face looked older than Arthur remembered. Sitting down, Geraint Morris took the sixty-year-old's hand in his, patted it softly.

– He's gone Arthur. I'm sorry.
– What – ?
– He passed away.

Until this point in his life, Arthur had a perfect facility with tears. Now however, the skill eluded him. Instead he stared dry-eyed into space. Geraint Morris thought of putting his arm around him, thought better of it.

*Be with him. That's all you can do.*

Arthur left the hospital at last. Bridget and Lilly had insisted on taking him in for a few days at least, but he would have nothing of it. He wanted to return to his own home.

Light was fading when he got back. Michael's last meal still lay there on the table, untouched. Arthur gathered saucers and plates together, piling them straight into the sink. Finally, he paused, panting. This is just the start of it, he thought. Up there, in the bedroom, were all his son's clothes. Then the bed, the sheets, warm still, maybe –

– No. Please God. Don't think of that.

And so Arthur went into the front-room, sat down beside the dark ashes of last night's fire. Night was advancing, slow, comforting. Arthur felt in his jacket-pocket for his pipe. Then he noticed something gleaming in the dimness. He bent low to forage with his fingers beneath the chair where Michael used to sit. Finally he held in his hand the hollow shell of a stainless-steel Timex wristwatch. For a moment there was a blankness. Then the old man recalled the text of a local newspaper, read at that same front-room fireside, several months before.

*The victim's black, fur-lined gloves and stainless-steel*
*Timex wristwatch have still not been found.*

No. Not possible. An odd coldness went through the man.

At about three in the morning, Arthur woke from a dreamless sleep. He rose, dressed, went briskly down into the garden. It was pretty hard work to remove that heavy Penlan boulder, but the old man eventually succeeded. He waited for the moon to go behind a thick cloud, threw the broken watch into the depths of the well.

# *Descent*

> The Thirteenth Station. Jesus is Taken Down from the Cross.
> "O Mother of Sorrow, for the Love of this Son;
> Accept me for thy Servant and pray for me . . ."

Just one year later, Geraint Morris recalled, the woodmen came. In the course of one long hot summer, the men worked with their axes and ropes and chain-saws to take Penlan woodland away. Each evening there was a church-like odour of burning leaves and stems which caught in everyone's throat. They cut down everything in their path, those men, even the huge beech trees whose existence went back, it was said, to Georgian times. Now those proud trunks lay like so many foot-soldiers, left dying on a field of blood.

The men worked efficiently with tiny transistor-radios balanced on hazel branches playing Beatles hits like *Please Please Me* or *I Wanna Hold Your Hand*. After a while people ignored them. They seemed always to have been there, mopping their brows clean of sweaty sawdust as the sun set purple beyond thick wraiths of smoke. But when these people were finally gone, the world suddenly knew like never before what they had done. For the cheerful rhythm of all those saws and axes had left a place of silence, emptiness and utter desolation.

Geraint and Zina looked. They looked again. But still they couldn't quite take it in. How could such a thing have happened? Yet this was a time long before Conservation and Green Politics. It was all so easy. Suddenly, you glanced up from all the bustle and busyness of your life and saw that dry, lifeless plain which had once been Penlan wood. It wasn't just the trees. Everything, every bush, every flower, every bird, every insect! The earth was warm still from the woodmen's campfires when the doctor one day walked along what had once been a shady forest track and found himself weeping uncontrollably for the dank, wing-fretted twilight which was no more.

The Forestry Commission left picturesque borders of young oak and ash, along with the birch-clad slopes on the far side of the stream. A cursory gesture, but also practical, for these would in due course act as wind-breaks. Within, over years to come, would grow those spindly conifer trunks, hundreds, thousands of them in dull mathematical order, banishing light and life from the earth.

A pine forest, Geraint Morris learned, is the quietest and coldest place in all the world.

Eventually, time did its healing work and he forgot. Yet sometimes, years after and at dead of night, the doctor lay in bed with a tangle of leaves and tendrils creeping across the carpet, triffid-like, to engulf him in a scent of aching loss. The man woke, snatched vainly at those curling fragments of places and people, before they were burnt to a haze of sunset woodsmoke, leaving only the echo of a tinny Lennon-McCartney chorus-line.

*I wanna hold your hand!*

Arthur stayed on at Ivy Cottage. Geraint Morris saw little of him after the business of Michael's death was over. He knocked on the door a few times, but never got a reply. A village boy would bring weekly groceries, now, leaving them on the doorstep. A filthy banknote was pushed by an unseen hand through the letterbox, in payment.

Whole years went by. Geraint Morris still made the odd visit, knocking vainly, peering through small gaps in the curtained windows. He imagined all sorts of things, but actually saw only the dark. A man from the Electricity Board gained entrance once, after threatening the Law. He said it was *one hell of a mess*, with the old man wearing filthy pyjamas even though it was two in the afternoon.

One night in the mid-seventies there was a call from the local police. Geraint Morris arrived to find Ivy Cottage's front-door open at last. The old man lay in those same torn night-clothes on the kitchen floor, wheezing painfully. His left leg was broken in two places after a fall. The doctor applied emergency splints, fighting a rank odour of ancient tobacco, unwashed clothes and cooped-up desolation. He noticed as he worked that every kitchen surface was piled high with yellowing papers, covered in a faded and mottled Remington script:

*To the Ministry of War*

They became friends of a sort again after that, although Geraint Morris never quite got used to the smell as he entered the house. Bile rose, hastily swallowed. The old man offered him a place at the kitchen table as he poured morning-old tea into two ancient, cracked cups. Then they would talk, although to be more precise, the doctor would mainly listen. For Arthur, it emerged, had a tale to tell, Ancient-Mariner-like, whether the world wanted it or not. That tale was Michael's Passion.

Geraint Morris heard it many times in the months that followed, but on each occasion the old man's swirling monologue, counterpointed by the whistle of a National Health hearing-aid, alighting upon some new intimate detail. The doctor felt a web of fascination forming, trapped in that sad, stinking room. Before him, the filthy tea-cup, the single stale digestive, lying on Medievalish yellow oilcloth. Such were Arthur's social offerings! Yet this was not about politeness, the doctor knew. No, this was ceremony, liturgy – sacrament even, with one name chanted over and over, soft and mystic. *Michael . . . Michael . . .* Young innocent, born so portentously on Christmas Day. Symbol of hope and strength and vision. But then, years later, destroyed in a tapestry of horror and violence, like that other December-born creature brought to Calvary to die upon the Cross.

*Will they ever come to cut him down?*

A hour-and-a-half later, dusk falling all around, the doctor walked briskly out of the house, hearing cold tea-leaves draining noisily down Arthur's outside-drain. The man strode through the gathering night, cleansed, elated by a brute relief. Not quite, however. For Arthur's Ancient Mariner narrative could never be quite exorcised. A painted ship, upon a painted sea, it lay

there, becalmed, until the day came when the doctor found himself returning once again to Ivy Cottage, despite himself.
– You can't help him, now, love.
– I know, Zina – it's just –
– Well?
Geraint Morris shrugged, looked away, said nothing.

The doctor was hard at work in his darkroom when the news of the fire came a few years later. Had the poor, demented man really tried to destroy himself and his home? It certainly seemed like it, if the police were to be believed. They told him they had to enter Ivy Cottage with breathing apparatus and more or less prise the old man from a burning arm-chair. Arthur was alive, just, and rushed to hospital where he was placed in Intensive Care. The next day, when the fire eventually got dowsed, firemen noticed a pale, humanish shape left on the back of the scorched chair – where Arthur had been.

A few days later Geraint Morris visited the place for the first time in a while. Above Arthur's wicket-gate, Penlan hill was sulky-looking, under an oppressive August sun. The fifty-year-old doctor stepped forward and suddenly glimpsed it, with a tremor of surprise. Ivy Cottage. Just weird jags of black between fronds of green. Where were the shutters? Where were those white-washed walls? Had the fire done all that?

Dr Morris advanced, found himself standing at what had once been Ivy Cottage's front-porch, today a mess of re-smelted iron and charred brick. Far away, a roar of motorway traffic. No more steam-shunters, mine-ventilators, foundry hammers. Just that monotonous hum of petrol and diesel, racing from nowhere to nowhere. Geraint Morris dug his hands in his pockets, turned to survey the rest of the scene. There was the rose-trellis, the swing-seat, the old well with its decrepit awning. The doctor almost expected to hear Michael's tuneless humming, but no, instead there was now a rush of warm Welsh air everywhere and the beech branches above his head began to hiss like some mighty Atlantic.

Then something strange happened. For, as this sudden wind rose, it seemed to take hold of all the ashes that were once Arthur's house and send them high into the air, whirling about the man like a blizzard. Just as quickly, the wind dropped, the ashes fell; and the man stood dumbfounded as the entire garden began to be covered in a fine blue-grey. Geraint Morris saw something lying at his feet. He bent, plucking a tiny fragment of charred paper from the path. There, unburned, a few faded, typewritten words:

*I shall dedicate my entire life*

Dr Morris turned, walked swiftly from the spot.

A few weeks later Arthur was well enough to be moved from hospital to a nursing home on the leafy outskirts of Cardiff. Geraint and Zina visited the old man in the glowing vividness of a September afternoon. The front-door was opened by a smart young man whose matching tie and blazer seemed to have very little to do with age and disease. Yet his smile seemed pleasant enough, ushering them both within. The couple found themselves standing on a stretch of gleaming parquet, the air filled with the smell of French polish. In the distance a pale oblong which was the day-lounge entrance, where a blue-clad figure stood, beckoning politely. The doctor and his wife approached. Odd, bespectacled faces looked up from old Country Life magazines and clumps of pastel knitting. Finally they reached the nurse.

– Relative?

Geraint shook his head.

– Just one of my old patients.

Pointing, the pretty young woman indicated a sunken shape silhouetted against a set of French-windows. Geraint and Zina passed through the day-lounge's sea of chintz-covered armchairs, parchment faces looming on all sides. There he was, finally. Poor old Arthur. Eighty-three years old, and, the doctor knew clearly at that moment, with very little time to live.

They sat down beside him. Zina took his hand in hers. Arthur's body seemed to be in the process of dissolving into the contoured folds of his chair. Yet there, at the heart of this slow-motion disintegration, was a pair of glinting pebble-lenses and behind them, those same, liquidish eyes which had experienced so much.

Now those swimming pupils rose slowly to meet Geraint Morris, began a laborious process of recognition. The doctor tried some well-worn words of comfort

– A good place – one of the best! – they'll take good care of you –

Arthur was far beyond such politenesses, however. Was it the doctor's imagination, or did a sad smile twitch fleetingly across those thin, broken lips? With sudden inspiration, Geraint leant forward, found a bony shoulder, gripped it emotionally. Those wafer-thin lips were moving now, he saw, tobacco-stained teeth making the beginnings of speech. The doctor moved his chair closer, put an ear next to Arthur's mouth, finally discerned husks of words

*Those stairs he came down – Fourteen of them! –*
*like Stations of the Cross*

Beyond the french-windows, chaffinches were conversing softly upon the nursing-home's smooth, privet-lined lawns. A murmur of afternoon chat-shows came from the day-lounge TV. Somewhere from the kitchens, an echoey Beach Boys falsetto. It was then that Geraint Morris remembered the early April day Michael had died and how those pills that killed him had trailed all the way down from the bathroom to the hall.

*Of course. It even happened at Easter*

Inside his head there was a scornful scream, like a sea-gull trailing lazily across a West Welsh cliff. Broken finger-nails seemed to dig into muddy scree for very life. Zina's voice finally brought the doctor back.
– What it is Geraint?
– Nothing.
A few minutes later, the couple found themselves once more before the man with the matching blazer and tie.
– Everything alright, is it, sir?
The doctor nodded hurriedly. Outside there was a smell of fallen beech leaves which made Geraint Morris momentarily want to cry.

A week later the doctor came back late from a home-visit to find his answer-machine winking in the gloom. He was making tea in the kitchen when the voice of that man with the blazer drifted up to him from the hall.

*Passed away peacefully in his sleep*

Geraint Morris put the hot kettle down carefully. He sat there in the dark. The sound of the river was louder than ever.

# Rest

*The Fourteenth Station. Jesus is Laid in the Sepulchre.*
*"My buried Jesus!*
*I kiss the Stone that encloses thee.*
*But Thou didst rise again the Third Day . . ."*

A year later Dr Morris made what was to be his very last visit to Ivy Cottage. Standing at a warped and paint-cracked wicket gate, half-open for all eternity, the man silently contemplated Arthur's home. Few signs now of the fire which had ravaged the house – except that one or two of the nearest beech branches petered out next to the roof in dark, charred stumps. Elsewhere the builders and decorators had done an excellent job on the building, even made one or two judicious improvements, for example replacing Ivy Cottage's old-fashioned stone guttering.

There was a disturbing new element, however, which Geraint Morris did not take long to pin down. Painters had transformed Arthur's continental shutters to an unnatural supermarket pink. It seemed a bad joke, those great blobs of pastel across the traditional white-washed facade. What would Arthur and Violet have thought? The doctor looked down at the Estate Agent's leaflet which he was carrying. A twinge of guilt went through him. He pulled himself together. Why not? Should the place stand derelict and lifeless forever?

The doctor wandered up the garden path until he stood beneath one of Ivy Cottage's tiny bedroom windows. He looked up. Yes. That was where Michael slept, facing north, towards the mountain. The doctor remembered then the storm of ashes two years before and the piece of typed paper he had found at his feet. But there was no rush of wind today. Life had moved on, hadn't it, endlessly renewing? Geraint Morris leant against a whitewashed wall, opened his old thermos.

It was then, gulping down a comforting draught of tea, that he noticed the swing-seat – or rather the neat pile of planks which was all that seemed to be left. Someone, probably a local builder's labourer, had meticulously disassembled all of Arthur's hand-made struts and trellis-work, laying them in a pile next to a coffin-shaped oblong of dark earth where the seat once stood. The weather had got to the wood, for now tiny fragments of paint lay everywhere, the doctor noticed, like showers of green confetti. He approached, crouched low. Idly smoothing his fingers across a piece of decayed planking, he suddenly felt the impression of a carved shape amongst the knots and gnarls.

An old crow squawked high above. For a moment the doctor's mind was dark as a cave. Then in a rush he knew the meaning and saw in his mind's eye the boy whose long fingers that had worked there, so patiently, with the blade of his father's pocket-knife – choosing the underside of the seat where no-one would ever look.

Poor Annie. He never forgot her.

Geraint Morris stood up, hesitated. Should he take it home? A memento, perhaps, a way of honouring the past?

– Hello.

He turned, jolted. Who was that white-haired woman at the gate? Those blue eyes seemed so familiar. She approached, smiling.

– Bridget, remember?

Of course. Violet's sister. The doctor shook her hand warmly.

– I'm staying with Lilly and the children. I always come, every year.

– Still living up there in Yorkshire?

She nodded.

– My husband died. I wanted to come home to my roots. But you get too old to change your ways in the end, don't you?

The doctor sighed, nodded. There was a patter of rain about them. Then, it seemed, a whole storm of drops. Luckily Geraint

Morris had brought his large black umbrella. They both stood under it, near what was once the cottage porch, sheltering. It was cosy, suddenly, as if they were very old friends.

– I have to confess – I was thinking of buying this place.

She gazed up at him, surprised.

– Now that the children are grown up and I'm retired. Zina and I thought it might be nice to be closer to Penlan hill.

– Really? Well go on, then – do it!

He stared at her.

– You don't think it's wrong?

– Why?

– I don't know – after what happened.

– People live, suffer pain, keep trying to be happy. Were they so very different?

She was right, of course. They lapsed into a silence. The rain thundered heavier and heavier, making everything unreal, including those vivid lapis lazuli eyes. She was glancing up at him, now, curious, a little timid.

– What is it?

– I've always wanted to ask you, doctor – you know, as an expert –

– Well?

She looked away, fumbled with her handbag. Then it came.

– Did Michael really do it, like Arthur thought?

Geraint Morris felt a tremor go through him.

– You don't mean Arthur actually believed – ?

Bridget was pulling out a tiny pocket-handkerchief, twisting it nervously in her fingers.

– The boy wasn't with him, that night, you see – not the whole time anyway – of course there was the question of the van and the body – Michael was no driver after all, was he? – but then when my poor brother-in-law found that broken wristwatch right there in the front-room –

Geraint Morris's skin turned ice-cold.

– The dead girl's watch?

She nodded, still staring down at the handkerchief.

– Michael was asleep in his room that night, most probably – but poor Arthur could never quite be sure – you know how it is, don't you?

They looked at each other. Geraint Morris felt the question coming despite himself.

– So Arthur must have lied to the police?

Bridget's fingers paused, frozen. Finally she nodded. Geraint Morris stared out into the roar of the rain. It was impossible. Absurd. After everything that Arthur had said and done. Was he dreaming?

– So it's yes, then, doctor.

– What?

She was looking at him at last. Her face was pale and determined.

– The police told you. They had proof. That's why the poor boy went and died.

The rain seemed to be roaring inside his head. Would this trial ever end? Geraint Morris summoned all the strength and conviction he could muster.

– No. They had no evidence. I assure you, Michael was innocent.

Bridget gazed up at him. Dr Morris remembered a day some years ago when a sick woman's fingers had dug into his wrist and he had somehow been able to find the right words. Had he found them again now, with Violet's sister?

– Thank you, doctor. You are very kind.

Her smile was oddly child-like, he thought, as she turned away. The rain was relenting at last. The quietness of the landscape brought back something of their first strangeness. They shook hands rather stiffly. Then he watched Bridget wander away down the garden path.

# Epilogue

Geraint Morris died a few years later, a victim of lung cancer, although he had given up smoking those few daily cigarettes of his some fifteen years before.

When, two months on, Zina plucked enough courage to sort through her husband's personal effects, she came at last to that cluttered, dusty darkroom at the back of the house. Tearing away a pair of filthy blinds, she noticed a black-and-white Ilford print lying behind the developing bench, where it had been clearly lost many years before.

It didn't look at all familiar. Zina picked it up, tore off some more of the old curtaining, lifted the faded image to the light.

Her hand went to her mouth.

It showed a gangling nineteen-year-old with enormous ears, sprawled across a swing-seat, smiling. But it wasn't the form of poor, dead Michael which took the old woman's breath away. No. It was that patch of dazzling afternoon sunshine, reflected unexpectedly off an Ivy Cottage window, shooting its dart right through a beech branch onto that uncombed tousle of Michael's hair.

Had Geraint fiddled with the developing lights? Or perhaps some mistake with the fixer had send that unexpected shaft of whiteness across the page? Zina took the print right up to the window pane, checked a second time. There could be no doubt. It was sunshine alright, making that shape over the boy's head, just like those gold-leafed halos Geraint took her to see at the National Gallery many years before.

– Maybe it wasn't lost. Maybe Geraint hid it.

Zina felt awkward, hearing the sound of her own voice. Silence returned to the cottage. Just the murmur of the weir drifting through the rooms now, as always. Zina stood there for a moment, staring into space. Geraint was a rationalist all his life, after all. Maybe he had felt a little bit ashamed that day, leaning over his developing trays, thinking those same thoughts about the boy. Zina smiled softly at the memory of her husband, the way he always pushed his hair back from his forehead when he was struggling with an idea or a belief. The ripples of the river murmured still, on and on through the house and now inside her mind. Suddenly her husband's laughter filled the room.